Broadwater

JAC SHREEVES-LEE

First published by Fairlight Books 2020

Fairlight Books
Summertown Pavilion, 18–24 Middle Way, Oxford, OX2 7LG

Copyright © Jac Shreeves-Lee 2020

The right of Jac Shreeves-Lee to be identified as the author of this
work has been asserted by Jac Shreeves-Lee in accordance with the
Copyright, Designs and Patents Act 1988.

A CIP catalogue record for this book is available from the British
Library

1 2 3 4 5 6 7 8 9 10

ISBN 978-1-912054-57-2

www.fairlightbooks.com

Printed and bound in Great Britain

Designed by Fairlight Books

This is a work of fiction. With the exception of any public figures,
names, characters, business, events and incidents are the products of
the author's imagination. Any resemblance to actual persons, living or
dead, or actual events is purely coincidental.

CONTENTS

INTRODUCTION

Ricky

Every local kid knows. We're taught about it in primary school and with thick, waxy crayons we draw pictures and write about it. Bonnet-capped milkmaids with wide, yoked shoulders, dozy cows and yellow fields of corn, wheat and barley. Broadwater Farm was a working farm going all the way back to the eighteenth century. Stables, carts, cattle and harvests. Perhaps teachers hope that knowing this local history will give us some kind of pride, remind us of the industry that once took place here and make us think that we have some of it in us, that we belong. My primary school form teacher, Mr Jenkins, said that back in 1973, Broadwater Farm was the jewel in the crown of Haringey's Planning Department – it was a modern-day Utopia. Mr Jenkins made a big thing about the Farm's history. He said you anchor your life in your history, dig up meaning and reason when sometimes there isn't much motivation to be found. I prefer to find my 'purpose', as my dad would say, in the present and not in the past. Old people look back all the time. My Great-Grandma Willa was always looking back. She was a strong woman who outlived her husband, her children and most of her friends but Mum said she had her head on back to front.

'Remember Lot's wife, look what happened to her,' Mum warned. 'She turned into a pillar of salt. That's what looking back does for you.' But Great-Grandma Willa carried on looking back to Jamaica even though she had lived in London since 1950. She told me stories about living in Stoke Newington (or Stokey, as it was called then) and renting a damp attic room in a tall Victorian house belonging to the Vee sisters, who were French ballerinas. She spent many nights worrying about whether my great-grandad would come home safely from his long shifts at the old Tizer factory in Tottenham – his walk back often involved dodging gangs of Teddy boys wielding bicycle chains as they went 'nigger hunting'.

'You know, I never did feel I truly belonged here,' she said. 'White people are good at reminding you that you is a foreigner, no matter how long you stay here, how hard you try or how hard you work. They still ask third- or fourth-generation children where they come from even though those children were born here, have never visited Jamaica and couldn't even find it on a map. White people believe we is either to be feared or pitied, and time won't change that.'

Mum told her to stop the negativity.

'Not all white people are like that. Remember Rose and Vic Richie, Glenda Perham, Aunty Daisy... we've known some very decent, good and kind white people and don't you forget it, Grandma.'

But Great-Grandma Willa just kissed her teeth and flicked her hand as if batting away a fly. I always listened to her and, yes, I still miss her and her stories and the Paradise Plum sweets she kept in her pockets. It was the Windrush nightmare that broke her. She died under an avalanche of official letters, expensive visits to the solicitor and red tape that bound her mind, wrists and ankles. Most people in the neighbourhood know someone caught up in the Windrush mess, but problems like that go beyond the Farm. All the streets nearby have seen some kind of trouble and as my great-grandma used to say, everybody on the Farm and roundabouts has their own story to tell. Welcome to Broadwater Farm.

I

Teapot's Story

Three mice lie dead on a glue mat. Picking it up by the corners, Teapot avoids the sticky patch in the centre. He's been caught out like that before, glue sticking to his palms or fingers. After dumping the mat in a black bin liner, he places a new one near the back door. Mice creep in from the playing field, finding cracks in the petrol station walls. 'We're lucky,' his younger brother Kaz tells him, 'it could be rats.'

Teapot has spent the last few hours cleaning the shelves and surfaces. He keeps a big yellow bucket of warm, soapy water at his side but doesn't bother changing it when the water turns a dark, metallic grey. Dragging the mop over the once-cheerful yellow floor tiles, now defeated by time and reduced to dismal beige, he sighs. Kaz will moan that he hasn't rinsed the floor properly and Kaz will be right.

Corners have been missed and thin lanes left unwashed but once Teapot has thrown the dirty water down a nearby drain, he returns the bucket and mop to the narrow cupboard where the cleaning materials are stored. Dulled by the drudgery of selling petrol and convenience store odds and ends, his eyes scan the assortment of pointless have-a-nice-day knick-knacks on the counter, the tacky key rings with smiley faces, the 60s CDs that never sell and last Easter's chocolate eggs, going cheap.

The central aisles are stacked with groceries and the corner area near the door is filled with bottles of deionised water, brake fluid, antifreeze, tow ropes, blind-spot mirrors, emergency puncture repair kits, L-plates, turtle wax and a myriad of other car-maintenance materials.

There are cardboard air fresheners ranging from 'Old-Fashioned Vanilla' to 'Hot Sticky Fudge'. Teapot can't believe anyone would seriously want a car smelling of hot sticky fudge. It isn't a bestseller; customers prefer 'Lavender Fields', and supplies often run out.

There are sad bunches of droopy flowers left in the plastic tub beside the newspaper rack and men who have forgotten to buy flowers for their wives stop on their way home to rummage among them.

Some customers, like Mr Pettigrew, the polite old boy with skin the colour of mushroom soup, come to buy a Lottery ticket before the 7.30pm deadline.

Mr Pettigrew once told Teapot that he wants to leave Tottenham and return to his childhood home of Devon, where he'll end his days with sedate clotted-cream teas and views of an unchanging, unhurried sea. Others are hooked on what they could do with a cool hundred million rollover.

Tariq Ali, better known as Teapot, and Kazim Ali, known as Kaz, have worked in the petrol station since leaving school. Local kids call them the Petrol Brothers. Their father says the family business is a 'good little earner'. He hopes his sons will continue with it, but Teapot's mind isn't set that way; he has ambitions and dreams above the stink of petrol and carloads of unhappy families. Five years earlier, just after he left school, Teapot found a job with a summer playscheme and enjoyed it even more than he'd expected. He likes lippy, hell-bent kids and can spot the fear and doubt beneath their gritty bravado. During the first week, one boy, Panayiotis Christodoulou, popped a small plastic peg up his left nostril and two days later managed to wedge his head between some railings. 'Crying out for attention,' decided Rob, the lead youth worker. Teapot found a way in and over the following six weeks turned Panayiotis into a boisterous, laughing eight-year-old. Rob told Teapot he was a natural with the kids.

And for a while he toyed with the idea of training to be a youth worker or teacher, until his father said, 'Forget it. No one makes money helping messed-up kids.'

When Teapot returned to college, Kaz asked if he was being serious, remarked that he needed his head tested. Kaz isn't academic; he prefers fast cars, women and the slick, steamy rush of nightclubs.

Teapot checks his watch; almost ten o'clock, Friday evening. Only the feisty, keen-eyed foxes patrol the local streets at this time. He likes the night, catching the edgy coil in the air, the scent of risk, of most people heading home but others intent on breaking whatever rules and taboos they keep in the day.

The thick glass door pushes open and a young black woman steps into the shop. Donna Flint.

'She walks in beauty, like the night.' Byron's words could have been written for her. Her black skin fleeced with the buff of midnight and the startle of her dark, baleful eyes. Each time she walks in, Teapot feels something new moving inside him. She comes in all weathers, arms either loose and swinging or tightly folded beneath her breasts as if she's bracing against a harsh wind or cramped with period pain. Donna reminds him of no one else. She is purely and wholly herself, but in a trapped and belligerent way.

As she walks past the curved mirror mounted in the corner, Donna's figure stretches and spreads as she cartoons in and out. Teapot sees her lips move as she softly sings *dubadubaduba*. Picking up one of the awkward metal baskets, she hooks her arm through its red rubber handles. She never buys petrol. As far as Teapot knows, she can't drive, hasn't got a car.

Teapot went to school with Donna's brother Danny. In Year Ten, they'd bunk off school, head to Tottenham Marshes, smoke weed and fish in the nearby River Lea. They only ever caught small blue-grey minnows which they always threw back. After the Tottenham riots, Danny got sent down along with Eddie and Big Mikey, his cousins. It was Danny who coined Tariq's nickname. Other kids called him half-breed or mongrel, but with Danny Flint he was just Teapot.

Never given full membership by black or white kids, Teapot was pushed to the periphery. He tried not to let the other kids matter, but back then Kaz carried a small, ivory switchblade.

Donna walks along each aisle, armoured in her denim bomber jacket and narrow jeans. Multicoloured bracelets join the jingle-jangle percussion of metal basket and high-rise heels. Hovering over the jams and marmalades, she stoops to search through the biscuits, her fingers fluttering over the Jammie Dodgers and Jaffa Cakes.

After tossing a packet of Maryland Choc Chip Cookies and a bottle of Irn-Bru into the basket, she quickly drops two packets of custard creams, her favourites, into a jacket pocket.

Sometimes she steals small loaves of bread, bottles of shampoo, bars of soap or packs of processed cheese from the fridge. A couple of times a week, in this small fluorescent theatre, Donna performs her deviant ballet and a watchful Teapot wonders what she'll steal next. She reminds him of a bad magician he saw as a kid at a friend's Halloween party, where nobody clapped and everyone spent most of their time on their hands and knees hunting for a lost white rabbit.

Donna tucks a stick of Cadbury's Flake up her left sleeve. She's needle-thin and he's curious about what she does with all that food. Some years ago, he went to Danny's eighteenth birthday party and there was a very long kiss that in Teapot's head ran into miles and hours. Teapot had slowly opened his eyes to peer at Donna's glorious face and there she was looking back at him. She broke off the kiss and left him in the hallway, confused and stranded. Later he got it. You don't peek when you're kissing. It raises a suspicion that your motives are elsewhere or that you're second-guessing. Teapot, however, had been fully present – so present he thought he'd combust. Donna continued to ignore him for the rest of the evening and he assumed he'd been filed under 'mistake'.

Afterwards when they passed one another on the street they'd mumble awkward hellos that drizzled into sheepish, barely-there nods. A handful of years now cordon them off from that night. Teapot has emptied his time away in the petrol station and Donna disappeared for a while. People said she went to stay with relatives in Derby.

Crouching by the fridge, she squeezes a small carton of milk into another pocket.

Local gossip reported that she wasn't well; something whispered, half-caught, 'women's problems' or something 'mental', when the world went wonky or she went wonky in the world.

Teapot wonders whether life has stolen so much from her that she wants to snatch it back. She's a bit strange in her inwardness, he thinks, but she's also a bit of wonderful, torn-tinsel Tottenham. He doesn't know when Donna's fingers became so light and nimble, but he guesses there are empty inside pockets that she needs to fill.

She lands the basket noisily on the counter. Scanning the items, Teapot punches keys in the cash till, aware that from behind her beaded curtain of dreadlocks she's watching him. Each time she moves her head, her golden hooped earrings sway across her cheeks. He doesn't know what she sees, worries about his feeble efforts to grow a 'poet's beard'.

'Suits you,' she comments, staring at his chin. 'I like it.'

She's chewing gum, her mouth slack, giving him a flash of white teeth and candy-pink tongue.

'That'll be five fifty,' Teapot says, looking up and locking his eyes on her face. His voice softens when he speaks, shrinks to the back of his throat; he coughs in the hope of restoring some authority, but it just buckles and breaks.

Donna counts out loud and gives him a handful of coins. The dark cupboards of her eyes are filled with secrets and he senses something is broken.

'Four eighty, that's all I've got,' she says, wrinkling her snub nose, sizing him up, square in the eye. 'Can I owe you?' she asks.

'How about you and me hanging out together?' He coughs hard and his Adam's apple bobs like a stone he can't swallow.

'You mean like a date?'

'We could carry on from where we left off.'

'At Danny's party?'

'Yes.'

She swings her weight over to one hip and rests a hand on her waist. Pushing out her chest, she smiles and slowly a gate swings open.

'Okay. You got yourself a deal. Took you long enough to ask.' She laughs and he laughs with her. As she brushes her nose with the back of her hand, he glimpses the polished nails, chewed at the edges. It's the brew that gets him every time: the bric-a-brac of trial and error in her presentation; the worn high heels, buttons missing, locks tucked up and locks breaking free. And the sweet, musky perfume she wears underneath the cigarette smoke.

'Next Friday. Seven. I'll pick you up.' He wants it to sound like a decision, a done deal, but it comes out more like a question.

Her face breaks into another broad smile and she turns to leave.

'I'll be back later,' she calls out, without looking over her shoulder. Her hips work a swing in the way that some women walk when they know they're being watched or believe they've hooped a good thing.

Kaz strolls through the door just as Donna leaves. Without acknowledging her, he saunters up to the counter, tugging the slim cords of loud, pumping sound from his ears. Dark shades balance on his head. He's been to the gym, working out; dense muscles bulge like they might split open.

'Check this.' With a wide grin he flashes Teapot a shot on his phone. 'Tiny thinks she's out of my league, that I'm punching above my weight.' Kaz brings his phone nearer to

Teapot's face. 'Fit, innit? Met her at the Black Cat. You missed out there, bro.'

Teapot thinks it's easier to agree and nods, but he notes the quiet fretfulness tugging at the young woman's eyes in the photograph and her forced, unconvincing smile.

Like wolves, Kaz and his friends hunt in a pack. Teapot knows the sleight of heart Kaz plays with women's emotions, how he zeros in for the kill.

'I'd cut off my hand for a slice of that,' Kaz adds, then presses 'save' and slips his phone into the back of his jeans.

Teapot heads for the toilets round the back, where the floor is wet with piss because some people are lazy and can't be bothered with accuracy or hygiene. The blue and white 'Now Wash Your Hands' posters point out the hazards of dirty hands but Teapot concludes that the posters are generally ignored by the punters who use the toilets. Washing his own hands, he glances in the mirror above the metal washbasin; his father's face, minus the odd gold tooth, stares back at him. He knows his father imagines him treading too closely behind, the weak-kneed, undeserving usurper. Every now and again Teapot's father reminds him that he can still show him a thing or two and that 'there's life in the old dog yet', while bopping around him swinging punches.

Back in the shop, Teapot takes out his paperback of poetry from beneath the counter. The book refuses to lie flat and keeps turning inwards after being squeezed in his pocket. He has homework; an essay on the Romantic poets, Byron, Shelley and Keats. John Keats once lived just down the road on Church Street in Edmonton.

Teapot visualises him living in the present day, hanging out with the brothers. Swaggering and boasting along with everyone else about things he's never done, or sitting there quietly in the corner, committing them all to paper. Old J.K. Teapot likes poetry and stories, and while Kaz preens and parties, he shoots up on literature. It was Miss Pringle who gave him his love of poetry. He remembers her round mouth blowing out poems like smoke rings as if trying to enchant the class and take them on a word-spun magic carpet ride, but whenever Teapot glanced around the classroom most of the kids had nodded off.

Reared on his mother's Irish bedtime stories of wailing banshees, the children of Lir and the mighty giant Finn MacCool, Teapot revels in folklore, and even in adulthood he still holds out for a fairy-tale ending. In particular, he likes the story of how his parents met. Many years ago Farouk Ali met Siobhán O'Sullivan when they both worked at Thorn Electrics. Siobhán worked in the canteen. She never used to charge Farouk for tea and regularly gave him free sandwiches; that's how he knew she liked him.

Opposing the marriage, Farouk's parents warned him that his disobedience would earn him 'the chastisements of Hell', but Siobhán's parents welcomed Farouk's moneyed presence into their family and trod any private doubts underfoot. Siobhán stopped working after she married Farouk. The understanding was that he would take care of her and she would take care of their home and their children.

Teapot's distant grandfather had helped clear the dense Guyanese jungles for tea cultivation and then worked on sugar plantations. Whenever Teapot's father talked about the suffering of the indentured Indians, his mother would dredge up the Irish potato famine and the plight of the 'white niggers'. 'That's what they called us,' she'd announce proudly. Teapot wanted to tell her to stop showing off. Competition for the crown of the most oppressed would follow and then Jews, Palestinians and Africans would be poured into the mix.

'Blacks? My dad used to call them porch monkeys,' Teapot's father said. Kaz laughed out loud but Teapot left the room.

Teapot tidies the box of nylon tights that has toppled from a shelf and recalls his earliest memories of things intimate and warm. He remembers a Christmas, long ago. Laughter stopped when five-year-old Teapot entered the kitchen; the couple sprung apart as if suddenly scorched. His father said that he was helping Aunty Loll with something and dropped the mistletoe to the floor. Teapot thought his father had been eating his aunt, devouring her pretty doll face.

'Mummy told me to get a plaster.' Young Teapot held out his thumb.

'It's just a scratch.' His father shrugged and walked out of the kitchen.

Bending down, Aunty Loll took Teapot's small hand and led him to the sink where she held his bloody thumb under the cold-water tap and wrapped it in a plaster. He wanted her to kiss it better. Aunty Loll was soft and warm and made a kind of swooshing petticoat music when she moved. After that evening, she never returned to their house and his father began talking to Teapot without looking at him, sentences barked like slammed doors. Nowadays Teapot finds it hard to remember a time before the doors were closed.

Placing the box of tights on the shelf, he settles on the stool. Kaz returns from checking the petrol pumps on the forecourt.

'Studying again?' he asks, looking over Teapot's shoulder.

'Homework.'

'You need to live more, bro. There's a world out there and you're in danger of being left behind.'

'I'm gonna be a social worker, Kaz. This,' Teapot points at their surroundings, 'and all that clubbing ain't for me.'

'I got other strings to my bow too, bro,' Kaz replies, winking and turning to his phone.

Teapot opens his book on Byron.

A little later, Kaz asks, 'Did you fix the coffee machine?'

'Yeah, the wires at the back were twisted.'

The machine pumps out coffee with four simple commands; push, pull, pour and go. Next to the coffee machine there is a shiny new black microwave parked beside stacks of pies, pastries and baguettes ready for heating. Teapot often catches his reflection in the glass of the microwave door, one side of his face shrunken, the other skewed and sloping, staring back at him like a lovesick moon.

Aware of the boom-boom background bass of teenage cars surfing the streets and puncturing the late-night silence, Teapot turns a page of his book. The heavy door pushes open. Donna stands there in her high heels, her finger- and toenails freshly painted in stars and stripes, which Teapot suspects isn't about any particular love for the United States but a fashion statement, the latest nail thing. Her eyelashes are heavily draped in mascara and her lips purple and pouty with gloss. This newly painted face all for him. Offering Teapot a warm smile, she melts him to mush. He smiles back, but on spotting Kaz, Donna quickly turns her attention to the bread and pastries. Glancing over at her, Kaz pulls a sick face and mouths the word 'skank'. She walks over to the refrigerator topped with large unrealistic toy tigers and lifts a six-pack of beers. Swinging round, she stops and gazes down at the cosmetics.

Teapot studies her every move so as not to miss anything, however slight. She could take it all, the liquorice allsorts, the chocolate fingers, the loo rolls; the petrol could run out, every car could stall and he would still look on, hanging onto the poetry and promise of Donna's *dubadubadubas*. Below the slip of skirt, her dark-brown legs are bare, the muscles in her calves sinewy and taut. She is a gazelle, graceful and lissom, though he worries that in her high heels she might topple and break at any moment.

He wishes she'd kick off her shoes and dance towards him to whatever music she hears, his arms encircling her like strong rope.

He waits for another smile.

Walking towards the counter, Donna looks directly at Teapot, fixes on his shy, gentle eyes and the sleeping snake of his black ponytail. After scanning the six-pack, he looks up and holds her gaze. He could never wink properly and instead offers a soft smile.

'Seven pounds,' he says.

Donna produces a five-pound note and some change.

'It's okay,' Teapot says.

Narrowing his eyes, Kaz shakes his head. 'No, it ain't okay. No wonder the figures don't add up if you're giving stuff away.'

Ignoring Kaz, Donna looks at Teapot. 'Thank you,' she says and turns to leave.

Kaz blocks Donna at the door, watches the smile falter on her face.

'Where do you think you're going? I think you've got something else to pay for.'

Donna hesitates.

'Well?'

Gripping an arm, he shakes her. The six-pack falls to the ground along with two bottles of glittery pink nail polish.

'You think you can come in here and take what isn't yours? You know what my pop calls people like you?' He digs his fingers into her arm.

'Fuck off.' Donna pulls herself free.

'Sewer rats. Dirty. Filthy. Sewer rats.' Kaz thrusts his chin forward, hardens his eyes and sniffs the air like he smells something bad.

Leaping over the counter, Teapot runs towards the door.

'Enough,' he says. 'Just leave it.'

Looking at him, Kaz says, 'Not fucking likely. She's a fucking tea leaf. And it ain't the first time, is it, bitch?'

'I said leave it.'

Kaz stares long and hard at Donna. 'Go on, get out. Don't show your face round here again. I mean it.'

Teapot pushes open the heavy door.

'You okay?' he asks her softly.

Donna's dark eyes are wet and she bites down hard on her bottom lip but manages a faint 'Thanks.' Slowly, she walks out into the night where heavy clouds choke the moon and stars from the London sky.

Closing the door behind him, Teapot turns to Kaz. 'What is it with you?'

'With me? The woman's a thief. The world don't need no thieves. Her whole family's trash. Everyone knows it. Her brother's inside, her mum's a crackhead.'

'Shut it.'

Kaz points a finger at Teapot, stabbing it in the air.

'I don't get it. Do you fancy her? Donna Flint? You've got to be kidding me. She's a thief.'

'And you're so different?'

'This ain't about me.'

'So the speakers don't count?'

'The riots were something else. You don't get it. This place is ours, our yard. She was stealing from us.'

'That's where you're wrong, Kaz. I do get it. Tottenham people are us. All the people with shops on Tottenham High Road are our people. Mustafa. Dennis. Rahul. Mrs Parker. Bobo and Chikodi, the guys in Roots Muzik, who you and your mates looted the speakers from. They're us.'

'No. They're not us. I know where to draw the line.'

'The line? What line? Do you seriously think politicians and feds see a line?'

Kaz doesn't answer.

'Well, they don't. In their eyes we're all the same. You. Me. Dennis. Mrs Parker. The guys from Roots Muzik. Donna. We're seen as the small, unimportant people. When the haves look at us, they see the have-nots. The never-gonna-haves. It ain't about this poxy petrol station. The picture's bigger than that, but you don't see it, do you, Kaz? You don't see how we're all in this together. We've got to change things, turn it around.'

'God, you're so sad. All this shit about change. I'm not one of your small, unimportant people.'

Teapot shakes his head. 'Look, I'm not saying we're small or unimportant. What I'm trying to say is we're on the same side and we've got to stick together, fight for the same things. You, me, Donna. You think working in this petrol station makes us bigger pieces on the chessboard? Gives us any kind of real power? Do you? Then you're more lost than I thought.'

'Fuck you, Peter Perfect!' Kaz shouts, spit sparking from his mouth. 'Don't preach to me, I know how the world works.'

'Yeah, sure you do.'

Kaz's eyes bore into Teapot. 'You think you know how it all works, you and your fucking books, but you don't know shit. All that poetry of yours don't mean nothing in the real world.'

For a moment Teapot thinks back to when he and Kaz were kids fighting over a toy fire engine, his father cheering them on. This row is about all their yesterdays as much as it is about the here and now. The rabbit hole goes deep; their fight is a thousand years old.

'I know who I am, Kaz.'

'You? You know fuck all. You really think your dead poets and your dumb degree are gonna change anything? Well, newsflash; they ain't.'

Looking around, Teapot draws in a deep breath, his voice raw and ragged. 'This place ain't gonna amount to a pot of piss. It's just money, petrol and more money and more petrol and that's it. It don't mean anything and it ain't ever gonna mean anything. You. Dad. Look at it, it's just quicksand. That's what quicksand does. It pulls you under, leaves no trace. It doesn't grow anything good, it doesn't change anything. If you're not careful you'll sink along with everything else round here.'

'Quicksand? What the fuck are you talking about? Your problem is that you think you're better than me and the old man, with all your smart-arse words and your flash ideas.'

'I never said that.'

'You didn't have to. I know one thing; you can become

the biggest fucking poet of all time, it ain't gonna change a bloody thing.'

'I can try. I don't want to be like you or Dad. I want my life to mean something.'

'Well, you can dream on all you like, but the petrol stink's on you, it gets on everything round here. You need to wise up, Teapot. It's dog eat dog out there. This is us. This is who we are and this is what we do.'

Kaz keeps his eyes firmly on Teapot's face but Teapot fixes his eyes on the endless stream of night-time traffic. Without returning his brother's gaze, he says, 'Like I said, quicksand.'

As he places the beer back in the fridge and the bottles of nail polish on the cosmetics shelf, Teapot's steps sound loud on the sticky floor. He sits down on the stool, its leather seat cracked open like a busted lip.

Kaz throws on his jacket and storms out of the shop, bad blood and anger raking through his face. Releasing a long breath, Teapot forces the exhaust and petrol from his lungs but his heart still hammers.

The following morning Teapot can't find the two boxes containing the speakers Kaz had hidden in the lock-up at the back of the petrol station. He makes no comment and leaves Kaz talking to a customer. Teapot knows where Donna works; Munchies on Tottenham High Road. He glances in, spots her in her sure-footed flats, dreadlocks tightly pulled back against her scalp, eyes dull with yesterday's menus. She looks short without her heels. No high-rise views here; her feet stand on solid ground and the *dubadubadubas* are silent in her mouth. Sitting at a window table, Teapot faces the full heat and glare of the morning sun. Dark, autumnal paintings dot the walls and although the chairs are new and comfortable, the wooden tables are old. The café is busy; soft-rock background music blends with the chatter of voices and the clink of cutlery. Donna notices Teapot and slowly approaches him.

'About last night,' she begins. 'I want to say I'm sorry.'

Teapot shakes his head and stops her. 'I'm sorry all round,' he says. 'Kaz should never have treated you like that.'

Neither says anything for a while.

'What can I get you?' she asks.

'Egg and chips.'

'Fried?'

He nods.

With a small black biro, Donna scribbles Teapot's order on a tiny notepad. She wipes down the surface of the table and glances at his book.

'Poetry?'

'Yeah, I'm doing an English poetry module, part of my foundation degree.'

'At CONEL?'

'Yeah.'

'My mate Debs goes there. She's doing hair and beauty.'

Teapot looks at her. 'What about you? What do you want to do?'

'Dunno.' She fiddles with her fingers. 'Still trying to work that one out.'

Replacing the biro and pad in a pocket, she says, 'Got to go. The boss will think I'm skiving.'

'Next Friday then?' Teapot asks.

She smiles. 'Yeah. Friday.'

Donna walks over to the kitchen and hangs Teapot's order on a small metal hook, alongside a row of other hooks nailed into the wall. The kitchen is hectic with spluttering appliances and orders being called out for collection. In her arms, Donna balances four all-day breakfasts for the long-distance lorry drivers, their eyes glued to the flat-screen TV.

From his pocket Teapot produces two slender bottles of glittery pink nail polish and puts them on the table beside a packet of custard creams, a five-pound note and some loose change. Donna works her way round the tables, carrying trays of hot food and warming drinks. Teapot catches and throws back the tentative smiles she sends his way. This, he thinks, must be the silly bliss of poets. Keats would understand and so would Bob Marley. In his notebook, Teapot writes that while poetry drills away at the marrow, it is other people who do the mending.

II

Mawusi's Story

The antibiotics had knocked Mawusi sideways and she was already hung-over when she walked into the Saracens Head. The pub was near the corner where Tottenham High Road leads into Bruce Grove. It had been refurbished with new windows and fresh bottle-green paint, but still smelled of boozy, musty odours that soaked the air and set up stubborn home in the fabric of creaking furniture. It was quiz night and the man calling out the questions asked about a Robin Williams film. Perched on a bar stool, Mawusi looked over at the team nearest to her, where a woman who was bawling out answers sat at the head of a long wooden table.

'Yessss... easy peasy!' the woman shouted, banging her fists on the table. '*The Fisher King*.' She cheered when the point was awarded and whispered something to a man with a Mohican sitting beside her. When the woman laughed Mawusi caught a flash of silver stud in her tongue. Wavy red hair hung in thick strands against the woman's forehead, and Mawusi thought she looked like a beached mermaid.

'What you looking at?' She glared at Mawusi, her green eyes beading.

Mawusi shrugged and turned away.

'You're not bad,' the woman told Mawusi later that night over cool glasses of lager. Her name was Julie. She winked and wiped her mouth free of froth. Mawusi laughed, noting the small starry scar above Julie's left eyebrow.

Two months later, Mawusi moved into Julie's flat. The flat was cramped and dark; sometimes they had to keep the lights on during the day. Mawusi carried her life in a small black bag and told Julie she travelled light.

'Bit of a drifter, are you?' Julie asked, grinning. 'Like Mary Poppins? Ha. Practically perfect in every way?'

It was the twitchy dance in Julie's eyes that Mawusi liked – this and Sammy, Julie's fat, gurgling baby. On their first Valentine's Day, Mawusi bought Julie a sterling-silver charm bracelet, carefully threading a mermaid, a treasure chest and a horseshoe onto the small links. The charms were chunky pieces but were decorated with fine, delicate detail.

'It'll bring you good luck,' Mawusi said, fitting the bracelet on Julie's wrist. In return, Julie had Mawusi's name tattooed on her back. The 'M' was crooked and although the tattooist had drawn a heart-shaped garland of leaves, he had forgotten the roses – but Julie couldn't see her back and Mawusi said, 'The colours are great, Jules. And the lines, he's kept in the lines.'

Gladys Pringle lived at the other end of Higham Road, in a terraced house with long, yawning windows and terracotta flower troughs. One morning, leaning against the garden gate, Gladys watched Mawusi walk past pushing the buggy.

'Morning,' Gladys said.

'Morning.'

'Cute baby. Pretty as a posy.'

'Yeah.' Mawusi struggled to hear Gladys's soft, quiet voice. It was pressed beneath the sound of passing traffic and the woman didn't raise her volume. She had a long, narrow face and steel-grey hair scraped back in a straggly ponytail. There was a thoughtfulness in her expression that Mawusi noticed was regularly broken by easy laughter. With bright, round eyes, Sammy gazed at Gladys.

'What's her name?'

'Sammy. He's a boy.'

'Oh, a pretty boy, better that way round than him being a girl and people asking "What's his name?"'

Mawusi chuckled.

'We live at number eleven,' she said.

Gladys nodded. 'They're great when they're this age. Don't answer back, can't give you any cheek.' She smiled at Sammy, gently stroking his tight, round fists.

Their exchanges of 'good morning' grew into longer chats and invitations inside Gladys's ground-floor flat for coffee and pink-yellow wads of Tottenham sponge cake. The living room was filled with untidy stacks of books, newspapers, magazines and journals.

Gladys said she hated ignorance, liked knowledge. She told Mawusi she used to be a teacher.

'Year Nine,' she said and pointed to a large framed photo in a bookcase. In the photo a younger, sandy-haired Gladys was surrounded by a group of uniformed children. 'Bless them. I bump into them sometimes. Still call me "Miss". They've got kids of their own now. The school gave me a family. I was the mother hen and those kids were mine every weekday from nine to four. It can be hard when you're adopted like me, you keep looking for a ledge, somewhere to take root or call home, but I've learned that belonging is about people, not places.'

Mawusi didn't consider it cheating when Gladys first pressed her lips against hers, sucked the hard nipples of her small brown breasts and fingered the dark pelt between her legs. Unlike Julie, who left love bites and scratches, Gladys's touch was tender.

'You're just sharing, Mawusi, spreading the love,' Gladys said. 'Think hippy. Jules doesn't have to know, no one needs to get hurt.'

Afterwards Mawusi always found money in her pocket. Twenty- and fifty-pound notes. They never talked about this.

The first time Mawusi brought money home, she tossed the small pile of crunched-up notes on the coffee table.

'Where'd you get that?' Julie asked.

'Glad.'

'What, she just gave it to you?'

'Yeah.'

'Just like that?'

'Yeah,' Mawusi said, tugging off her jacket.

Julie raised her eyebrows. 'Well, if she's mug enough to give money away, who are we to stop her?'

She reached out to Sammy who was sitting on his activity mat. He started whimpering and crawled along the carpet until he found Mawusi's leg, then clung on tightly.

'Suit yourself,' Julie said, frowning at Sammy. Mawusi took a long time folding away Sammy's clean clothes and didn't eat the fish fingers and baked beans Julie had cooked for dinner. She said she had lost her appetite.

Sammy was growing fast and needed nappies, clothes, food, toys. A quick crawler, he often got stuck under or caught between furniture. Mawusi opened the official brown envelopes that came through their front door most mornings. She ensured all the bills were paid and kept a careful note of incoming and outgoing money, but their welfare benefits soon ran out.

They cut back on eating out and it was strictly Lidl and Poundland for shopping, although Julie said prices were creeping up now that Lidl was trying to attract a more 'upmarket' kind of customer. She managed to get a job at Superdrug but Mawusi couldn't work because someone had to take care of Sammy and they'd agreed that the first person to get a job would take it and the other would stay at home to look after him. Julie had got hired first and she said to Mawusi, 'You're better with Sammy anyway, more maternal.'

Whenever Mawusi brought Sammy to Gladys's flat, Gladys would move piles of books and the dining table to the far side of the living room to clear a space on the carpet. After covering the area with a creamy fleece blanket she had bought from Mothercare, she'd scatter a selection of toys for Sammy to play with; noisy, gum-friendly rings with bells, soft fabric balls and a demonic robot that violently shook, rattled and rolled, blinking on and off. Mawusi thought Sammy was a bit young for the robot but thanked Gladys anyway. She was grateful for the gifts and the money.

'What have we got here?' Gladys said, holding up a big teddy.

Sammy babbled, showing chips of white teeth, but cried when Gladys brought the bear nearer, burrowing his face into the crook of Mawusi's neck.

Mawusi allowed Gladys to hold Sammy, dangling him on her knees while playing 'bumpsy daisy' and feeding him bright yellow eggy soldiers.

'I took early retirement a few years ago when I was fifty-five,' Gladys said. 'I was burnt out. That's secondary school teaching for you.'

Mawusi sighed. 'We used to give our teachers hell. Three boys chucked Mr Blenkinsopp, our French teacher, out the window and poor Miss Woodruff got locked in the music cupboard. Most of them were supply teachers. Factory fodder, one called us, before she walked out of our classroom in tears.'

'Did you get any qualifications?'

'Art. GCSE. I really like art.'

'You should do a course.'

'I can't, not with Sammy. I'd like to do design, fix things up, make things better.'

'You could start with this place,' Gladys said, pulling a glum face as she looked at the living room walls. The wood-work was chipped and the white paint yellowing. 'It needs a serious makeover.'

'It's got character.'

'That's a polite way of saying it's dated.' Gladys laughed. 'This place is like me, old. Maybe I'll let you work your creative magic after I've earned a bit of money.'

Gladys sat Sammy on the floor and handed him a squeaky rubber tractor.

'Thought you said you'd retired,' Mawusi said.

Gladys handed Mawusi a mug of black coffee and offered her a plate of chocolate digestives. 'The pension doesn't go far.'

'What do you do then?'

Gladys paused and then said, 'Clinical trials.'

'What's that?'

'I lend out my body to pharmaceutical companies.'

'Really?' Mawusi dunked a chocolate biscuit.

'Yes, they test new medications, different viruses, new strains of infection, diseases and so on, and they assess my reactions.' Gladys winked. 'I'm giving medical research a helping hand. It's called altruism.'

Mawusi frowned. 'Sounds creepy.'

'Not really, it's all pretty matter-of-fact. There are no age limits and – let me think... I've done about nine in the last three years. You're only allowed to do three a year. Last year I helped out on chronic obstructive pulmonary disease – COPD, to those in the know.' She sniffed. 'I'm doing a flu camp in a couple of weeks.'

'Whereabouts?'

'Northwick Park, but I've been to Coppetts Wood, Wembley, Milton Keynes, central London, everywhere.'

'How long for?'

'Depends. I've been gone for three days, sixteen days at the most.'

'Bit risky, innit?'

Gladys sat up. 'No, it's all low risk. It's like being in a hotel. You get fed and watered. There's a telly and you stay on a ward or in your own room, but it's all comfy. And you meet lots of people. I met a man who'd made enough money to buy land back home in Bulgaria and there was a woman who wanted to start a pet-grooming business. Some people don't want to talk, and it's best to leave that sort alone because you never know.'

'I hope they're paying you enough.'

'Last year I earned twelve grand.'

'You having a laugh? Twelve grand?'

'Well, thereabouts. You have to sign a form and everything.

And there's follow-ups, you know, outpatient visits once you're discharged, but there's nothing to it really.'

'You're a human guinea pig, Glad.' Mawusi sipped her black coffee.

'Guess so, but we need human guinea pigs. Yellow fever was only stamped out because a group of volunteers agreed to be test subjects. How else do we get rid of diseases and make the world a safer place? We have to give to get something back.'

'Not always. Some people just take.' Mawusi looked down into her coffee. 'Sometimes it's not so straightforward.'

'No, not just sometimes. Life is never straightforward.' Gladys half-smiled.

Before Gladys went for her next clinical trial, she gave Mawusi a set of keys. At the end of the week Mawusi popped into the flat to feed the goldfish and water the rubber plants. When she told Julie about Gladys's clinical trials, Julie shook her head and said, 'How can it be okay for someone to take a small dose of something that kills people in big doses? Doesn't add up.'

'Well, that's how vaccines work.' Mawusi shrugged. 'Glad says it's one of the best ideas of modern medicine.'

'I'm not so sure.' Julie tilted her head to one side. 'When you think about it, it's really sad, innit? In fact it's more than sad, it's wrong. Lonely old soul like that, having to rent out her body. You can see how old people get taken advantage of. It's horrible getting old and wrinkly. Most of them are on their own. I mean, look at her, she's got no one to love her, not properly, not like a partner or a lover. You're the nearest thing she's got to family. She probably sees you like a daughter. Thank God she's got you, Musi.'

Mawusi didn't say anything.

'Well, whatever she says about modern medicine, I wouldn't do it.' Julie narrowed her eyes. 'Hiring out your body – God knows what they put in you.'

'Who knows what's inside any of us?' Mawusi added quietly. She stood up, saying she would check on Sammy who was sleeping in his cot.

When Mawusi arrived at Gladys's flat on Monday afternoon, she found her sitting in an armchair watching *Cash in the Attic.*

'Hello, stranger,' Mawusi said.

A thick mohair coat covered Gladys's body even though it was a muggy July day.

'It's summer, Glad. There's a heatwave and you're wearing your coat?'

'Nice to see you, too. Come here, lover.'

She held out her arms and slowly Mawusi walked over. Sammy was asleep in his pushchair; Mawusi lifted him up and laid him on the fleece rug. Studying Gladys, she noticed that her cheeks were sunken, her face gaunt. Bones jutted from her frail body but Mawusi loved those sharp edges that didn't cushion her character. As she licked and kissed Gladys's skin she thought she detected the taste of vinegar. In the warmth and tumble of her bed, Gladys turned to Mawusi and slowly traced her profile with a finger, moving it slowly along her forehead, the deep bridge of her nose and the soft fullness of her mouth.

'I look at you and I see Africa and all its beauty,' Gladys whispered.

'Ghana. My family is from Ghana. Africa's made up of fifty-four countries, Glad. I don't look Tunisian. Africa has many faces.'

'I know that. I just want to celebrate your beauty. Beauty is everywhere and it's in everyone.' Gladys leaned closer, kissed Mawusi's mouth and gently bit her lower lip.

Mawusi jerked back. 'Don't do that.'

'I'm sorry. I didn't mean to hurt you.'

'You didn't. I just don't like being bitten... you know, it's weird but white women always bite me in bed. Why is that?'

'All white women have bitten you in bed? When you make love?'

'Yes, actually, a lot of them have. Jules does.'

Gladys shook her head. 'I don't know, I can't talk for Jules or other white women.'

'I read somewhere that biting's a form of ownership, marking one's territory, branding.'

'Come on, Mawusi, maybe it's not that sinister. It could be just the lovemaking style of some people, whatever their colour. Their sign of affection. Maybe the white women you've mentioned bite all their lovers, not just the black ones. Perhaps it's not about ethnicity or race at all.'

'Not about race, Glad? When isn't anything about race when you boil it down?'

Mawusi shifted her body and brought her face close to Gladys's.

'I mean, what do you really see when you look at me? Something exotic? A bar of chocolate? Something on which to leave your mark?'

'Hey, come on. I can't not see you as black and you can't not see me as white but the chocolate stuff, putting a mark on you, it's not like that with us.'

'Isn't it? Isn't it always like this when people like you and people like me try to connect? Race raises its ugly head and spews out all the rubbish that comes with it. You're always talking about things happening on an unconscious level. Perhaps love and sex cause deep unconscious stuff to surface all the time but we just don't want to admit it. You may not want to face it, but stuff is there, it's always there.'

'You know, I was listening to *Woman's Hour* yesterday.'

'Here we go,' Mawusi said, letting out a big yawn.

'The guests were discussing gender, sexuality, identity and a concept they called the heteronormative narrative.'

'Enough with the big words, Glad. Honestly, sometimes it's like being back at school.'

'But that's just it, we're outside of all of that, you and me. We make love, we care for one another and that's it. The world's definitions and bullshit stop at the front door. This is what love looks like.'

Mawusi rolled her eyes. 'A love that transcends race and racism, really?'

'Yes, really... You know, if I could give you the world I would. You mean everything to me, Mawusi.'

Mawusi didn't stay for dinner. She wanted to see Julie before she left to start her shift; she'd got a new job at the bookies. Closing Gladys's front door behind her, Mawusi found five hundred pounds neatly folded in her jeans pocket. The notes were new and crispy between her fingers. She decided she would treat Julie to a chicken vindaloo at the weekend.

Mawusi had noticed a chemical smell that was barely there but, like a senile dog, followed Gladys from room to room. When she visited a fortnight later the smell was stronger and Gladys looked weaker, stooping as she walked. She kept coughing, and Mawusi decided not to bring Sammy with her next time.

'I'm not feeling too good,' Gladys said.

'Do you want me to call the doctor?' Mawusi asked, jogging Sammy harder on her hip than she realised. He squirmed in her arms, wanting to climb down.

'No, I'll be all right. I called the nurse at the unit and she said I've just had a bad reaction but it'll pass. She thinks it's a post-trial virus, nothing to do with the actual trial.'

'She would say that. I wish you'd let me call the doctor.'

'Now who's being the mother hen? Stop fussing, I'll be fine. Please. This has happened once before. Bad reactions. You get them every now and then. It's part of the package.'

'It's not right, Glad.'

'What is?' Gladys turned up the television volume and the broken faces of refugees fleeing Burundi filled the screen.

Mawusi looked away. 'I can't stay, Glad. I've got to get back. Need to put the dinner on and give Sammy his bath.'

'Course. Think I'll go back to bed.' Gladys switched off the television, blew her nose and limped back to her bedroom. She didn't put any money in Mawusi's pocket, nor did Mawusi find any behind the clock on the mantelpiece where Gladys usually kept it.

Mawusi wasn't sure where the five hundred pounds Gladys had given her went, but when she added up the grocery shopping, the bills and rent paid, the curries and Chinese takeaways, Julie's hair extensions, Julie's false nails and Julie's new gym membership, it was all accounted for.

On Sunday, Mawusi left Julie and Sammy at home. It was raining heavily and the dirty grey sky looked as if a giant greasy thumb had smeared its surface. She walked the length of Higham Road and turned the key in the front door to Gladys's flat expecting to hear Radio Four. Intelligent, talking, mind-growing radio, Gladys called it. Boring was what Mawusi called it. But the flat was silent. Gladys was sitting up in bed. The bad smell was getting worse; it hung around the flat like a third person.

'I've got this funny taste in my mouth,' Gladys said. 'I've tried everything to get rid of it but it won't go.'

Climbing onto the bed, Mawusi wrapped an arm round Gladys's shoulders, touching more bone than flesh.

Gladys said that her body felt as old as iron and that spending too much time sitting around feeling awful had warped her mind, making her think of death and endings. In a quiet voice she said that for a brief moment she had even thought about forcing open the clocks' dials and removing their hands, but then she chided herself for even having considered spoiling their perfect, polished faces. Yesterday she'd managed to take down a mirror and remove two clocks from her living room and bedroom.

She had been able to leave her flat and walk very slowly to the local Oxfam shop where she'd handed in the clocks and mirror along with her wristwatch. On the way home she had bumped into Miles Campbell. He'd nodded and shuffled by.

Gladys remembered Miles Campbell from former parents' evenings; his son, Harley, had an astonishing acting talent. No, not his son, she corrected herself. Conjuring the teenager's face, she told Mawusi that one afternoon Harley had stayed behind in her classroom and told her about being transgender, a girl lost in a boy's body, unable to tell her father. Gladys turned to Mawusi and whispered, 'I wonder how Harley is now, and if she's loved.'

The feel of Gladys's skin was papery and cold. Swollen blue veins buckled on her wrists. Mawusi's fingers tracked the circular depression left by Gladys's watch.

'It's funny, isn't it?' Gladys said, suddenly sitting up, her eyes starry. 'Before I met you, I thought I was finished, that there wouldn't be any more surprises, that I had done all the living I would ever do. Then you came along and hey presto, I'm a different person. It's like I've grown a new heart, been born again, given new eyes, new ears. Ha. Everything's brighter, bolder and more beautiful. It sounds cheesy but sometimes cheesy's true. Love means you can't go back to who you were. Love's a conversion.'

She looked into Mawusi's raisin-brown eyes and added, 'My adoptive mum was a born-again Christian, you see. In her church people were changing all the time, being born again. Right now I wouldn't mind being born again, I mean properly, a nice new body. But my mind's still all right, I think.' And she laughed, coughing and spattering into a bundle of white tissues.

'God, Mawusi, look at me. Weak as a kitten and talking nonsense. Ignore me.'

'You're all right. You never talk rubbish, you're the educated one, remember?'

Gladys managed a feeble smile. 'I feel rough, but I'll be okay. I always am,' she said, squeezing Mawusi's hand.

In a quieter voice, she asked, 'You a bit low on money, love?'

Mawusi nodded.

'There's money on the mantelpiece. Take what you need.'

As Gladys turned and climbed out of bed, Mawusi spotted an ugly, mottled scab spreading across her back like mould. Standing up, Mawusi dressed and decided to add a capful of Dettol to her bathwater when she got home. She pushed the odd notes she found on the mantelpiece into her pockets. Gladys followed Mawusi into the living room, pulling the woollen dressing gown around her tall, lean frame and said with surprising strength in her voice: 'That's a worried face if ever I saw one. What you thinking? Time to jump ship? It's okay, love. It can't be easy. I get it, I really do. I never expected you to stay. Look at the state of me. And look at you and all that young apple beauty. I never expected anything more.'

'It's not like that, Glad. I've just got to be getting back.'

With watery eyes, Gladys gave Mawusi a smile as wide as the horizon. 'Of course you have.'

Mawusi turned to go. Her black jacket felt tight across her back. Leather has a way of stretching and shrinking like a living thing.

'I'm not sure when I'll be back, Glad,' Mawusi said, her voice breaking. 'What you said about people changing and love being a good thing, you were right.' She left the door keys on the small table in the hallway. 'I'll come by when I can.'

Gladys nodded. 'When you can, love, when you can.'

Before she left the house, Mawusi knocked on the door of the upstairs flat. Will, Gladys's neighbour, opened the door, a bowl of pasta cupped in one hand and flecks of tomato sauce in his pale, frothy beard.

'Glad isn't well. She won't have it but I really think someone should call the doctor.'

'Thought she looked a bit peaky,' Will said. 'Leave it with me, I'll sort it.'

Heading downstairs, she quickly closed the front door behind her. It wasn't chilly outside, but Mawusi zipped up her jacket all the way to her chin. She hurried down the road, waiting for the money to turn bad in her pockets. When she arrived home, she found the television on and Peppa Pig's face filling the screen. Julie and Sammy were asleep on the sofa, their heads close together as if sharing a dream. She walked quietly into the bathroom and peeled off her clothes. A pile of crumpled twenty-pound and ten-pound notes fell to the floor; she covered them with her T-shirt. Fishing Sammy's rubber tractor and yellow duck from the tub, she placed these with the rest of his bath toys in a blue netted basket.

Mawusi turned on both taps and poured a full bottle of Dettol into the steaming hot water, then stepped in, keeping her head down and steering her eyes away from the reflection in the mirror.

III

Miles's Story

Slumped in worn, sunken armchairs, Miles Campbell and Trevor Blackwood take swigs from chilled cans of beer while watching *Sounds of the Sixties, Seventies and Eighties.*

'Remember when we used to go raving down Hammersmith Palais? The Fatback Band?' Miles asks, guzzling a long swallow of beer.

'Yeah. Wicky Wacky.' Trevor starts humming and moving his arms in a sitting-down boogie. 'Man, now that's what you call some badass tune. *Hmm, hmm, hmm, bababadabadadabaa.* Oh yeah, that was a cool tune, man.'

Miles likes sixties sounds best, especially Sonny and Cher. A young Cher slinks across the television screen, kohl-dark eyes fastened on the camera, her body sheathed in a black, wet-look catsuit. She lowers her head and sings doe-eyed.

'"Bang Bang". I used to love that song,' Miles says. 'Pure vintage. That came out in 1962. She's seventy-three years old, you know. Saw her in a magazine, don't look a day over forty.'

'Yeah, thanks to her cosmetic surgeon,' Trevor says, lying back against flattened cushions. 'I like my women natural.'

'You mean you like rolls of flab, bitching? Periods? Moods? All that natural woman stuff?'

'Yep. All of it. I love women just as they are. I wouldn't change Maria for anything. If I want plastic, I'll buy a blow-up doll. Got to keep it real, Miles. Plastic's toxic.'

Trevor and Miles used to spend Wednesday afternoons at the senior citizens' club in the West Indian Cultural Centre in Turnpike Lane. When Miles Campbell, Trevor Blackwood and Reuben Riley played dominoes, they would win, lose and become seventeen again.

Young black boys in 1970s Britain. Ackee-seed black. Tottenham black. British black. Fighting skinheads and dodging Doc Martens black. Young and vital, looking up at the stars. Used to call themselves 'the Three Musketeers'. They still recall the jerk in their jeans, their dip and fall-back sugar-cane swank, sweet-talking pretty girls with pram wheels turning in their eyes who yielded like melting butter.

'Mona? Mona Warwick? Chut, man, now dat was some woman... Lord have mercy... Remember the jugs on dat? Dem were the days, nuh?'

Miles, Trevor and Reuben. North London yoyo kings. Soul boys. Reggae boys. Rude bwoys. At the West Indian Cultural Centre they would eat ackee and saltfish, patties, curry goat, fried dumplings, cow-foot stew and drink mannish water. And the hotter the pepper sauce, the better. Licking their fingers, last-dance memories in their talk, they'd roll back the years.

Now Wednesday evenings are spent in Miles's flat where the men watch television and chew the cud. Miles lives behind the Cultural Centre in a new block of flats built where old chocolate factories once breathed cocoa into the Wood Green air.

He likes Marcus Garvey Lodge but the walls are thin and he's careful about keeping the television volume down. Reuben is spending time in Saint Vincent with his cousin and only two of the musketeers remain, Miles and Trevor, who talk about people they used to know, the old gang.

'Chalky died,' Miles says, dry-eyed.

Trevor nods. 'Yeah, I know. Cancer.'

'Prostate cancer. They caught it too late.'

'Yeah, I know.'

'We're one point six times more likely to develop prostate cancer than white men.'

'That's what the stats say.'

'Now why do you suppose that is?'

Trevor shakes his head. 'I don't know but you're sure as hell gonna tell me.'

'Vitamin D deficiency. It's all down to vitamin D,' Miles says, folding his arms like he's fixing up to talk business. 'A capsule a day keeps cancer away.'

The television screen changes and KC and the Sunshine Band belt out 'Give It Up'.

'Now what year was that?' Trevor asks, scratching his chin as KC gyrates in tight turquoise trousers.

'Dunno. Eighty-two? Eighty-three? Round about the time Otis left for Canada.'

'You mean *had to* leave for Canada.'

'Yeah. Scary times.'

As if there are others who might overhear them, Miles and Trevor lower their voices when they relive the night Otis got away with it. Otis is Trevor's cousin. Years ago he committed a stupid crime, a break-in at a local grocery shop; it went wrong and someone got hurt. No one died but money was stolen, and afterwards everyone kept their heads down while the Old Bill poked around. Before he left the country, Otis asked Miles to look after his gun; he hid it in a sock behind a wardrobe. Otis never returned to the UK so Miles kept it.

A Beretta 92 pistol. Miles didn't feel he'd perverted the course of justice when vague, unreliable mugshots were shown on Crimewatch. He just waited for the years to go by.

He keeps the pistol hidden in different places, under floorboards, inside the toilet cistern, behind ancient volumes of the *Encyclopedia Britannica*.

'You should come back to the Cultural Centre, man. Everyone misses you. It's kung-fu season at the cinema club. Bruce Lee and Jackie Chan. Or what about the bingo club on Thursdays, or a game of snooker with me, Skippy and the other guys? Reuben will be back at the end of the month, he'd love to see you,' Trevor says.

Miles is silent.

'Come on, man. It's no good being stuck in here all by yourself. Life's for living.'

'I know that.'

'We have a laugh down at the centre, remember? You'd enjoy yourself.'

'I do enjoy myself. I like my life just as it is. I've outgrown the Cultural Centre, same old, same old. I like my life, Trev. Peaceful and quiet.'

'Loneliness is a killer, Miles.'

'I'm not lonely, I just prefer my own company.'

'Sure, sure you do.'

Miles walks Trevor to the front door. 'Hope to see you at

snooker. Think about it,' Trevor says, his face unlined despite the passing years. Miles nods and quietly bolts the door.

In the kitchen, he dumps dirty dinner plates, knives and forks in the sink; he watches them vanish under soapy water and decides to leave the washing-up until morning. He used to go to the cinema club on Fridays at the local Odeon where he'd watch spaghetti westerns; Clint Eastwood shooting bad guys after asking them if they were feeling lucky. He stopped going when the audience began shrinking. Buster died last month and Wesley the month before. The cinema club turned into a waiting room.

When he was younger Miles told himself that he wouldn't grow old; now he says he won't die. Death happens to other people. Like a bullet-sprayed Clint Eastwood, he'll dust himself off from whatever illness comes, stand up and shout 'That's a wrap.' He'll take every vitamin supplement he can and stuff the scythe down Death's throat. He'll be the last one standing, no matter what life throws at him, just like Clint Eastwood and Charles Bronson. Only he won't ask the bad guys if they're feeling lucky because he believes he's the lucky one, the deserving one. This is Movie Miles talking. The cowboy of Turnpike Lane. Black cowboys in the American Old West accounted for up to twenty-five per cent of all cowboys in the late nineteenth century – Miles has done his homework. His saloon is the Wellington Arms on the corner of Wood Green High Road and Turnpike Lane, and his no-good woman has left him.

He wants to tell Trevor to butt out of his business but they go back too far. Gunslingers don't need anybody and isn't Cher doing fine without Sonny? Time has taught Miles he doesn't need anyone; he is better on his own, behind a mortice-deadlock door.

When his parents emigrated to England, Miles was left behind in Jamaica. He was called a 'barrel child', as were all those boys and girls who waited for their stash of candies, toys and clothes sent in a barrel from 'foreign'. He could smell his mother's perfume, stingingly sweet, on the new clothes. He imagined her hands and fingers carefully flattening each item. Rifling through the clothes, he would burrow down into each barrel until his Uncle Moses asked him what he was looking for, but he couldn't tell him because he didn't know. With strong, seeking hands Miles pushed at the bottom of each barrel in the hope that they would give way and something wondrous would come pouring out.

On arriving in England, no longer a barrel boy, Miles discovered that the woman and man who greeted him at Heathrow airport were strangers and the baby his parents said was his sister had taken his place. He had never wanted to leave Jamaica and say goodbye to kind Uncle Moses and gentle Aunt Dorcas, but he had no say.

The narrow bottle of kananga water perfume sat on the edge of his mother's walnut dressing table; it didn't take much effort for him to knock it off so that it broke into little glass fragments and created a puddle on the lino. Miles felt the graze of his mother's eyes when he told her it was an accident.

'It'll have to come out of your pocket money,' she said. Kananga water reminded him of the mossy, woody, green scents of Jamaica, the sweet insides of a barrel – a barrel for a barrel boy. Even full barrels are empty, Miles decided and repaid his parents with truancy, poor school reports and low grades.

The weather forecast is now on television. A young white man in a sharp three-piece suit says he's been trying to think of a word to sum up the July day ahead; he decides on 'unseasonal'. The weatherman talks about the jet stream, says there'll be a 'chilly night ahead' and frost. Miles shakes his head – frost in November, that's to be expected, but frost in July? Sightings of snow in the Scottish Highlands? Farmers and sheep suffering? Miles figures there's a general decline, a gradual slip and slide all around, but not having a garden, he doesn't worry about shrubs or blooms being killed by frost. And what was that about a Super Blood Wolf Moon? That's a bad omen if ever there was one. But Miles doesn't scare easily.

Miles is only responsible for the small rooms of his one-bedroom flat. He lives on the third floor. There is no lift, and as he's grown older he's come to hate climbing the stairs and the way his increasingly frail hands clutch the metal handrail. A pushchair used to be parked outside flat twelve where the nice couple live but it hasn't been there in the last few months, nor has he seen or heard much of the couple or their baby.

He doesn't like to ask or poke his nose in other people's business but he's curious about the baby, the pushchair and the nice couple whose names he has forgotten.

Sometimes Mrs Hudson on the second floor invites him in for tea and biscuits. She'll say, 'Hello, Miles,' her small blue eyes twinkling in a grey face creased like throwaway paper. 'Fancy a cuppa?' she'll ask, and shortly afterwards he will find himself in her flat, playing handyman for all those things that need fixing. Last time he was there, he bled the radiators.

'What would I do without you, Miles?' she said. 'You've got a good heart.' And into his palm she pressed a slice of cling-film-coated apple crumble. Mrs Hudson has gone away and is visiting relatives in Leeds.

Miles knows all about relatives. Years ago, he had relatives, a wife and a son. His wife's name was Yanina but he called her Nina – everyone did. Sometimes he can still smell her, as if she's just left or entered a room; hers was a sweet, floral smell, the kind that clings. After they were married Nina tied herself to him, coiling tightly like a vine. Sitting there in her armchair, never far from view, she would wait and stare at him like a deathwatch beetle. She sat there most nights, not saying much, and he would frown at her as if she were a hefty piece of furniture waiting to be lifted.

Night after night Nina gave him dinners of tough overcooked meat but he pushed away her burnt offerings. Her family were from Aruba where the divi-divi tree grows. Divi-divi trees bend and flatten in the direction of strong trade winds and like them, Nina could only lean one way. She was boring and dull. When Nina talked about Aruba it was clear to Miles she didn't know what to leave behind. She wasn't what he wanted and neither was their son, Harley, with his foolish dreams.

'Dad, I'm going to be an actor,' Harley had said. 'Check this.'

Prancing round the sitting room and reciting rhymes, Harley threw out his arms like he was on stage. He told his dad this was a soliloquy from *Othello*. Miles watched, listened and scratched his head saying, 'Well, Shakespeare you sure ain't.'

Harley stopped. 'Miss Pringle thinks I've got real talent.'

'What the hell does Miss Pringle know about real life? All I ever hear is Miss Pringle this and Miss Pringle that. Damn interfering white woman. She doesn't know anything about us, about being black, about having to struggle. She just sits there trying to teach those kids when the vast majority of them don't want to be there, don't want to learn and have no discipline. I can't stomach that woman, she talks out of her backside, telling me about my son when she don't know jack shit.'

'You could try to like my acting, Dad.'

'You need to get a proper job, boy.'

Slowly, Harley closed his notebook.

'That's what you're best at, Dad.' Harley's eyes fell to the floor.

'What?' Miles said.

'Shooting things down, killing things before they grow.' Harley turned and left the room. Miles heard the sound of drawers banging and wondered what other trouble the boy was getting into.

Nina and Harley moved to Oranjestad, leaving Miles alone in London. He tells himself he was a good husband and a good father. He worked hard, never shirked his shifts with British Rail. Nina and Harley were wrong; they shouldn't have left. They betrayed him. Like duppies they visit his thoughts and teeter on the edge of his vision. He's heard Nina has returned to the UK to take care of her younger sister Manon. Nina would be good with dead and dying things, Miles thinks, visualising the square, ugly palms of her practical hands. When Miles remembers Nina and Manon, dried fruit comes to mind; brown fruit with hard rind for skin, the kind you spit out because it has no taste or flavour.

Just two days ago he almost walked into Miss Pringle but resentment made it impossible for him to say hello; the most he could manage was a nod. She looked so frail, holding tightly onto a walking stick as she entered a charity shop. It wasn't the first time he had seen her since Harley's school days. More than once he'd spotted her going into the library or getting on and off buses. And the black teenager with the baby whom Miles had seen shopping with Miss Pringle, laughing and joking as they stacked packets of Pampers into a shopping trolley – who was she and what was going on there? The girl looked like a boy. Another stray, he thought. The daft woman was obviously a collector of lost young souls.

Miles has kind of adopted Errol, the young man who lives upstairs on the fourth floor, in the flat above his own. Errol's a plumber; now there's a trade Miles believes in. He tries not to think about Harley, who never phones, never writes. He'd sought to help his son, to guide him, but he was made like his mother. The features of their walnut-brown faces have faded with time. Nina and Harley looked alike, birthed from the same dark divi-divi pod.

Errol has given Miles a key to his flat in case of emergencies like the time Errol's bathroom flooded. Miles likes it when Errol calls him 'Pops'. He pulls himself up to his full height when he talks with the younger man. He feels like he matters again, like he makes a cut in the world. Walking beside Errol, he thinks they would be even closer if he was young, like brothers. They'd share spliffs, laugh at the same jokes and fuck the same women.

In the living room, Miles turns off the television and draws the thick curtains; they snag on the rail until he pulls harder. Curtain-drawing is a habit. Nina used to say she was 'keeping the heat in', but it's summer, July – he shouldn't need to keep the heat in. They've predicted a chilly night though and the cold plays devil with his rheumatism.

Miles stares at his face in the round chrome shaving mirror. Spinning the mirror round, he studies his magnified self. He wonders what happened to the young black man who raced around North London believing he was special, would net life, wrangle anything. He'd drive through the streets in his white Triumph Stag, being stopped six times in one day by the Old Bill, who were always eager to take a wog down and make their quota.

Bastards.

The young man who never thought he'd get old, who believed getting old only happened to other people, looks at the old man gazing back at him in the mirror. He hates the snow in his hair. His true face is somewhere in between, must be. Miles's youth is a distant foreign continent; its exotic tastes have long since gone, and when he passes young people in the street, he hangs his head. He understands the workings of shame, how it alters one's gait, one's claim on the world.

Lying down on his bed, Miles closes his eyes. His head is woolly; he's drunk too much. As his breathing deepens he gives way to sleep, but suddenly there it is, the sound, the third time this week, and he turns over and groans. He can hear it clearly now; the rhythmic thudding like a strange tide surfing back and forth, back and forth, over the hill and down again, over the hill and down again, rocking to and fro. Gasps and cries. Everything is louder at night; each sound heard and made is amplified. Miles is reminded of farmyards where animals fuck whenever and wherever instinct takes them. He feels as helpless as a cow waiting for slaughter as Errol and his woman pound their bed and the ceiling shifts above his head.

Miles saw them last Sunday afternoon, fooling around in the car park behind the flats.

'Hi, Mr Campbell,' the woman called out, her mouth wide. Errol nodded. 'All right, Pops.' And Miles faked a smile.

The couple claimed they were washing Errol's car but all Miles saw was their goofing around with a soapy yellow sponge.

The woman's skirt was too tight, too short. Bending over, she dumped a black plastic rubbish bag in the litter bin. He felt the woman's eyes brush over his face, giving him a lazy 'whatever' look. She walked over to the car and leaned back against the bonnet like an urban sprawl, opening her smooth, brown thighs as Errol came slowly towards her. Errol whispered something and the woman grinned. Miles tried to look away. He should have warned Errol about women.

The thumping grows louder, filling Miles's bedroom. Like drumming, it has its own rhythm and the room rocks and shudders. He imagines their warm, wet bodies sliding against one another, their limbs twisting and tangling. Errol's body mounting and pushing into hers. Her body open, arched. Her soft, round breasts. Sweet-salty nipples. Miles slips a hand beneath his waist band and rubs hard at the swelling, his breathing growing hoarse. He can touch, smell, see, taste and hear their bodies as they force them down his throat.

Miles's breathing grows louder, more ragged, and then the noise stops. He freezes like he's been caught. He thinks he hears giggles. Have they heard him? Are they laughing at him? Miles imagines her face, her slanting, catlike eyes, the black braids against her damp forehead, the gash and sluice between her legs.

Bastards.

Miles throws off the bedsheet and marches into the kitchen where he grabs a broom that's propped against a wall. Returning to the bedroom, he lifts the broom and bangs hard on the ceiling. He waits and listens closely, but only silence answers back. He falls heavily on his bed, the ceiling pressing down.

Wondering what they're doing now, Miles visualises their brown bodies, their lust-swollen faces, smells the brine of their skin in the sheets. Errol's hands cup her warm breasts and a satisfied smile lights her face as she drifts into dreamland, spooned in sleep. Miles curls up in a tight ball and closes his eyes.

He hopes for sleep but the bedsprings start again, gently at first, and then back to their hateful rocking. Sitting up, Miles reaches for the broom and prods rapidly at the ceiling.

'Stop!' he shouts. 'For God's sake, stop!'

God? God? How does God come into this? What was it his father used to say before he took off his belt? 'I do this for your own good, son. You must abhor what is evil and hold fast to what is good.' Miles presses his hands against his ears but the pounding continues, becoming more insistent, decisive, until it is a battering, something being rammed home. The tightening in his crotch begins. Fingers and tongues. His head spins and tears slide down his face. Abhor what is evil. Hold fast to what is good. Hold fast to what is good.

Scrambling from the bed, Miles switches on the bedside lamp. He crouches down on his knees and thrusts his hands under the mattress, groping frantically around the tight space.

'Old friend, old friend, where are you?' he whispers and sighs with relief when his hands eventually grasp the gun. Bringing it to his lips, Miles smiles. People should get what's coming to them. It is natural justice like the kind dished out by the weather. The justice of a Super Blood Wolf Moon, its gravitational pull broiling his blood.

The moon will pull out the tides. If Miles was at the beach he would walk across the vast ocean floor just like Jesus walked on water.

There are at least three bullets. The noises from above grow louder and roar against his ears, drenching his bedroom.

Grunts, groans, cries, sighs. In his right hand he grips the spare key Errol gave him. Shutting the front door behind him, Miles climbs the stairs to the fourth floor. He forgets the metal handrail and his bare feet don't register the cold, hard flooring. One thought moves him forward.

He stares down at the black print of the word 'WELCOME' on the bristle doormat before turning the key in the lock and pushing open the front door. He fingers the cold metal muzzle of the gun in his pyjama pocket and walks slowly down the hallway towards Errol's bedroom. Miles was a young man once. Had a woman and son, buried his heart and body in them, tried his best. Turning the handle, he opens the bedroom door.

Bastards.

The air is wet with sex and wanting, dripping down walls and flooding the floor. It isn't very dark without curtains at the windows, and he makes out the hunched, moulded shape of their bodies.

Bastards.

'Mr Campbell?' Errol says, sitting up.

Calmly, Miles pulls the gun from his pocket. His hand is steady. The woman screams and Miles smiles. This is an honest scream; a clean, good scream.

'Hey, Mr Campbell, Pops?' Errol says, climbing down from the bed. 'Whoa… what's up?'

'This.' And Miles fires twice into the night. Bang Bang.

Everything is quiet. Miles wonders if time has stopped. He sits in a corner of the bedroom, turns away from the lifeless bodies and waits. When the police arrive, he hands over the gun. Baring his soul he tells them about being tied to a whipping post and how the couple provoked and tortured him. The policeman's heavy hand applies a solid pressure on Miles's head as he climbs into the back seat. This touch is impersonal, part of a bobby's everyday job, but it is the first time he has been touched in a long while and now Miles is grateful to be roped in with the rest.

Looking up at his bedroom, he catches a glint of the soft light coming from the bedside lamp. You'd imagine a nearby snuggling of warm bodies if you didn't know any better – but Miles does. His brown eyes dim as he turns away from the window, from the cold room and the fake light; the loneliest bedroom in the world.

IV

Ruth's Story

'Look at me, no hands,' Uncle Martin called, jollying along, and everyone fell in behind except Ruthie, who just watched. Uncle Martin's great square head surfaced from the plastic basin of water, a green apple held in his teeth – a Dunn's Seedling. Ruthie knew this because the apple was doughnut-flat, very green and hard. Her father had bought a bag of them only yesterday from the greengrocers, fresh in. Uncle Martin wagged his wet head like a shaggy dog; flecks of water like darts shot off from his hair and beard. The children splattered by the water laughed, and the laughter spread along their row of glee-filled faces like a running lick of paint. Ruthie watched. Uncle Martin spat out the Dunn's Seedling. 'See, no hands.' He waved his hands on either side and the children squealed, because Uncle Martin was the best apple bobber in Tottenham, the best apple bobber in the world. Ruthie turned away.

Years later, Ruthie wonders if she killed Uncle Martin with her thoughts, and she fears her thoughts have spun round. Thoughts do that, she believes, balance the sheets, give chase and catch you when you're not looking.

The car, a cherry-red Volvo, pulls up at the edge of a cliff. One hundred and twenty miles from London. Removing both hands from the steering wheel, Doug says, 'Look at that sky.' Sitting beside him, Ruth looks through the windscreen at the big sky; an unanswering sweep of blue.

'Isn't this the bluest sky you've ever seen? It's the bluest sky I've ever seen. God, it's blue.'

Ruth says nothing. Doug turns to her.

'Isn't it the bluest sky you've ever seen?'

'I'm not sure.'

'Are you kidding? They don't come much bluer than that.'

She unwraps the greaseproof paper containing the bundle of cheese and pickle sandwiches.

'When?' he asks.

'When what?'

'When did you see a bluer sky than this one?'

Shaking her head, Ruth says, 'I don't know.'

'So how can you be sure?'

She hands him a sandwich.

'I can't remember when I saw a bluer sky but I think I have.'

'Ha! That doesn't make any sense.' Like he's caught her out. 'You know that a lot of the time you don't make sense, don't you, Ruth?'

Biting into the bread, Ruth stares straight ahead at a blue pretender sky. Beneath her rough camel-hair coat is a forgotten hourglass.

'God, it's hot in here.' After removing his coat, Doug lowers his window. Cold air rushes in like an ice sprite. Turning, one knee digging into his seat, Doug reaches over to a back window and lowers it too until another cold blast of air enters.

'You do your side,' he instructs Ruth.

She places her sandwich on the dashboard. Unwinding the window on her side takes time; the handle is unwieldy and moves in jolting stops and starts.

'Here, let me do it.' Doug moves across her and forces the lever down, his face furrows and strains with effort. Wind whistles through the car and the road map on the dashboard flies off and lands flat, quivering against the steering wheel.

'That's better,' he announces, folding the map. 'Good. The sea air gets the body juices flowing. Getting away from it all – doc says it'll do us a world of good.'

Ruth pulls her coat tightly around her and wonders if she expected too much from life. Her mother warned her and her sister Binty: 'You'll only be disappointed, my dears. You expect too much from life and too much from men. They're just flesh and bone like the rest of us.'

Ruth's parents never made the mistake of expecting too much from anyone; they knew their limits and worked to a sensible, predictable routine. They always had the same dinners each week when Ruth was growing up, beef and carrots on Mondays, lamb chops, peas and potatoes on Tuesdays, sausages and mash on Wednesdays, and so on. Each week they bought the same items from the same known and reliable shops.

Ruth remembers Skinners shoe shop. She and Binty only wore shoes from Skinners. Memories of the smell of new leather and the sparkle and gleam of patent shoes came skipping back. Ruth loved buckles and bows once, a long time ago, before simplicity found a guileless place in her heart. Her mother's advice when Doug and Ruth first set up home was to the point: be sensible, penny-pinch but never scrimp on shoes, always keep your spoons and forks separate from your knives and the rest should sort itself out.

'You cold?' Doug asks.

She shakes her head and eats a mouthful of chunky pickle. 'No, I'm fine.'

'It's nice to get away from the flat, isn't it – and our neighbours?' Doug yawns and stretches. 'I like that Mr Campbell, he's a nice old soul, and Karen and Winston from the Farm, they're an inspiration, but Mrs Hudson's a nosy so-and-so.' He holds his sandwich in mid-air. 'When did you make this?' he asks.

'Last night.'

'I told you to make the sandwiches first thing in the morning. The bread's hard.'

Ruth continues eating.

'Maybe yours isn't stale but mine is,' he says.

She stops eating and offers her sandwich.

'No, thank you. I'm not hungry anymore.'

Doug returns his sandwich to its greaseproof paper and with tight fingers folds it into a neat, square package. The wind rattles the car. Winding up his window a little he looks out to the horizon.

'Do you think she was cold?' he asks.

Lowering her head, Ruth stares into the emptiness of her lap.

'In the morning, that morning when I went in there, her room was like a fridge,' he says, looking out at the cloudless sky. 'I asked the doctor... Only I wouldn't want her to have been cold. She was so small.'

Ruth drops the hard leftover crusts of her sandwich into a blue carrier bag, the thin corner shop kind that collapses when you reach the front door.

'The doctor said it was like she fell asleep,' Doug almost whispers. 'She wouldn't have felt anything.'

A fortnight ago they had the car valeted, as much to free them from the past as to clean its floor and surfaces. All dust, dirt and grime are gone but even now there are occasional breaths of baby; warm milk, sweet talcum powder and new plump skin. Just beneath the cover of today, a determined and painful register of who and what have gone before.

Ruth blows her nose and wipes her eyes. Some days the sky strains and tilts backwards as it is doing now, and she searches for somewhere safe and solid to fix her gaze.

'You catching a cold?' he asks, and fully winds up the window on his side. He swings round and, kneeling, reaches to hoist up the lowered window in the back.

'You do your side,' he says, but despite her best efforts Ruth struggles with the stubborn lever. He hands her a rattling can of WD-40 that he fishes out from under his seat and tells her to use it. After she's done this, the car is filled with the smell of kerosene.

'There,' Doug says, settling back into his seat.

The wind and cold air have gone; it is very still and quiet.

'Better now?' he asks.

She nods.

'Good.'

Ruth spots a small but growing cluster of fluffy white clouds forming heads, wizened men with shaggy beards that curl and twirl, billowing into cots and pushchairs, and now she's in the nursery, standing by Beth's cot, staring down at a bare white mattress and its layers of foaming memories.

'We need music. Let's have some music,' Doug says.

Fiddling with the radio dial, he transports Ruth back to an

earlier time when she bopped around on a dance floor, red, yellow, green flashing disco lights dizzying her teenage head.

'Beth liked music, didn't she?' Doug asks, but Ruth knows it is not a question. It is a reminder. Doug looks straight ahead, talks to the seagulls.

'Yes, the *Coronation Street* theme,' Ruth says.

'Funny that.'

'Yeah, funny.'

Ruth thinks of all the times when things described as funny are not funny at all, not when you filter them and look at what's left, the crystallised, indigestible truth.

It's not working, this tanking up with music, like Listerine failing to wash away alcohol.

'Perhaps not,' Doug says and twiddles the knob until Errol Brown stops singing 'You Sexy Thing'.

A wavy line of flapping, winged movement carves swirling shapes into the sky. Flinging itself downward, a seagull looms close and almost flies into the windscreen, but not before it stares in, eagle-eyed and bloodless.

'Do you think they have accidents?' Doug asks.

'I don't know.'

'Do you think things go very wrong on Planet Seagull?'

'I suppose so.'

'You suppose so... But you don't know, do you, Ruth? Like the bluest sky, you don't really know.'

Ruth stares out at the blank-faced sky, searching for clouds, while Doug delves into a large carrier bag by his feet and removes a handful of newspapers. He draws out several sheets: front pages, centre pages, back covers.

The randomly selected pages show a giant crossword

puzzle, glacial white teeth in a toothpaste advertisement, a footballer's winning goal, Boris Johnson on the way to Brussels, the daily horoscope readings for Capricorn, Aquarius and Pisces, Donald Trump on a podium, the oldest mother in the world and the details of an imminent railway workers' strike. Doug passes Ruth one of the newspaper sheets and keeps the others.

'Do your side and I'll do the rest.' Handing her a small roll of Sellotape, he sets about taping a page of newspaper against the window nearest to his seat.

'I'll do the back,' Doug offers and climbs into the seat behind. Tearing the Sellotape with his teeth, he seals the newspaper down. The last panel of glass to be covered is the windscreen and, as he does this, Ruth avoids the rushed movement of his hands and the stony concentration in his eyes.

'There,' he says, 'all done. Can't be too careful, you never know who might be walking by.'

Ruth can't ask what the point is and tell him that love can only ever hurtle towards its own end. She calls these her cudgel thoughts because they fall like killing blows, having the unwelcome power to render all moving images still.

Without the sun, sky, seagulls and sea filling everything with their sights and sounds, Ruth and Doug are locked in. The newspaper pages reveal a world outside hell-bent on turning, though mute and pinioned against glass. Doug settles into his seat; his hands unbuckle his belt and unzip his flies. He wriggles and pulls his grey trousers down. Releasing the lever by the side of his seat, he lies flat on his back.

'The doctor says we have to keep trying,' he says.

Blowing her nose, Ruth nods. 'I know.'

Newspaper print shuts out the sun, turning everything black and white. Ruth prises something open and is surprised that her mind works, that somehow ordered thoughts form silent words. A phantom cot hovers on the back seat and Uncle Martin performs terrible tricks with his hands. Soon the car will shudder, some kind of love will hit the sky and the hurtful weight of it all will be fantastically horrible, beyond measure. Doug has told her many times that she knows nothing, but one thing of which Ruth is certain is how glass feels when it breaks.

V

Winston's Story

'It should be worn in the middle,' Karen says, her fingers tugging the brass buckle to the centre of the belt. As if he's about to take a blow, Winston pulls in his stomach.

'Breathe out, Winston. You're not auditioning for a six-pack telly ad. Besides, Santas have big bellies,' she says with pins gripped at the side of her mouth, her voice tinny and tight between ventriloquist's lips. Relaxing his stomach muscles, Winston sighs and watches his wife's fingers fuss and fiddle with his costume, stitching and tucking.

'I told you to buy a new beard. This one's matted, must have got damp,' Karen says and drags a paddle brush through the long white tangle, taking much of the fabric with it.

'We're going to have to get you a new one for next year,' she says, shaking her head.

She rolls up her sleeves and Winston notices a cluster of red rashes on her white skin.

'Eczema again?' he asks, but she doesn't reply.

They're in the living room, the warmest room in their flat in Martlesham block. December has bitten with black-ice teeth. There is heavy snow outside. In villages throughout England

and Wales, people are cut off with power lines down and burst pipes. Despite continued weather warnings, the March of a Thousand Santas is going ahead. Winston meets his eyes in the over-mantel mirror. Cloudy, uncertain eyes, set in a drawn face the colour of teak.

Christmas cards stand sentinel on the mantelpiece; there's a small card from Mavis Browne which contained a generous donation, a large card from Ruth and Doug, who asked for support when their baby died, and another one from Mr and Mrs Norris who live on nearby Mount Pleasant Road. Mrs Norma Norris – God bless her.

Winston looks at the designs on the cards; a glitter-encrusted Christmas tree and the cheery faces of carol singers. He believes such Christmases only happen in snow globes, and even then only when they're shaken.

'Popeye was handing out leaflets about the community centre meeting this Thursday evening. Members of the council will be there. Hopefully we'll all be a bit clearer about plans for the Farm and what this regeneration actually means,' Karen says.

Winston listens, wonders what all their futures hold. The fleece moustache smells like stuff put away too long and itches against his skin. He untwists the tight elastic band that keeps the beard in place.

'Please keep still,' Karen says. 'I'm trying to sort this out.'

She circles him, her eyes travelling the length and breadth of his body. She moves closer to drag, pinch and yank at the material until her tuts lessen. The red velvet robe hangs about Winston's middling frame, but once buffeted with padding, his figure swells to Santa Clausian proportions.

There must be billions, thinks Winston, as he follows

the journey of the snowflakes falling outside the living-room windows. White inkblots of geometric beauty, each one a different configuration; cathedrals, temples, pyramids, palaces, new worlds. He loves Christmas and the silent lure of snowflakes.

'Don't think they'll make it to a thousand this year, what with the weather,' Karen says, her wide shoulders in alignment with the pointed right angles of her elbows.

'You can never tell with numbers,' Winston says. 'Some people start midway, others drop out. Some register online but never show. Last year I counted in at number 999, remember?'

Kneeling in front of him, a threaded needle hovering, Karen looks up. 'What does it matter anyway?'

'Well, this year I could be number 1000. The one who makes the difference. There's a big difference between being 999 and being 1000.'

'Not really.' Karen sniffs and returns to darning a hem.

'Might even be more than a thousand Santas. This year we could double it.'

'Not with this weather. Anyway, "thousand" is used in a metaphorical sense, they don't mean it literally.'

Winston doesn't expect Karen to understand; they often miss one another's meaning and he's learned to push down the hurt of her cool dismissals.

Their ten-year-old son, Robbie, died eleven years ago. Robbie's leukaemia proved too big to beat. He was cared for at Great Ormond Street Hospital where Winston first wore his Santa suit. With gratitude Winston abandoned himself to the baubled distractions of Christmas, smothering his fears beneath his Santa costume. He remembers young faces, bright-eyed in the face of death, dazzled by Christmas and his festive bodily spectacle. Lucy Paige's mother cried as Winston, ho-ho-ho-ing, handed her daughter a 'Barbie at the Beach' collection. Lucy's beaming, dimpled face was dominated by a plastic tube that ran along her cheek to her left nostril.

Winston arrived at Robbie's bed with his last Christmas present: a sturdy box covered in glittering Shrek-at-Christmas wrapping paper.

'Thanks, Santa,' Robbie said, winking, and tore off the rustling paper to welcome Action Man and his helicopter into the world. Robbie's Toy Story advent calendar sat on a white cabinet beside his bed. Pin-head perforations around the small paper windows had been punctured to display frosted Christmas trees and red-cheeked elves wearing conical green hats. Only six sleeps before Christmas.

Mrs Paige kept a vigil by Lucy's bedside and read stories loud enough for all the children in Dolphin Ward to hear. Robbie's favourite was *Ali Baba and the Forty Thieves*. He told his dad he especially enjoyed it when the boulder at the cave's entrance opened like a big yawning mouth to reveal treasure chests spilling over with topaz, opals, diamonds and sapphires.

He liked surprises and took to saying 'Open Sesame' whenever he was pleased with something. Karen collected his falling hair, locking the corkscrew curls in the trinket layer of her wooden jewellery box.

They were silent as they listened to the consultant, a pale-faced young man with a voice that dwindled and dried up at the edges. They were told it was a matter of time, a few more weeks. All they could do now was keep Robbie as comfortable as possible.

After the consultant stopped speaking, Karen and Winston left the room. Saying nothing to one another, they allowed the lift to carry them down to the ground floor foyer – the unreal portal where it had all begun. The hustle and bustle beyond the hospital was a callous blast to their senses. Karen talked quietly and vaguely, saying she needed to do some Christmas shopping. She didn't return home for four days. Winston told himself she wasn't missing and didn't call the police; he knew she was caught in a private blizzard. While she was away, Winston's worries gave birth to others like nesting dolls. He didn't eat, couldn't sleep. He told Robbie, 'Mummy has flu and can't come to the hospital until she feels better.'

Robbie nodded, wearing his toughened Action Man face. When Karen came home, she didn't bring any Christmas shopping with her. Winston never asked her where she'd been, and she gave no explanation. It was their last Christmas with Robbie.

They were encouraged to grieve, to mourn and to keep a memory box, which they renamed the infinity box, because what was time anyway? They had anniversaries and rituals like the Santa Claus tradition to keep Robbie and his memory alive.

'I wish you'd stay still,' Karen says.

'It's itchy.'

'Itchy or not, Winston, it'll take twice as long to mend if you don't stop moving.'

At last year's procession, Winston saw Santas he knew from previous years like Angus Fraser from Glasgow. He made Winston's sides hurt with his quick, cruel one-liners. Every other sentence, it was 'Eh, Winston, have you heard the one about...?' There were a hundred or so black Santas and a similar number in wheelchairs.

Years ago, one of the organisers suggested all the 'ethnic' groups stay together at the back, in front of the wheelchair users, to make a 'statement'. But Winston, the other 'ethnics' and the wheelchair users weren't happy about this and didn't want to make any statements.

'I know about racism in a way you couldn't possibly understand,' Karen said. 'You know about how racism is received, but I know how racism works, how it's done. I can beat the organisers at their own game. Watch me; I know how they think. I'm white, Winston, and I know what that means. A lot of white people don't recognise their whiteness, much less accept the privilege that comes with it.'

With determination marking her face, Karen wrote a damning letter and as a result there was no separation of the wheelchair users or black or 'ethnic' Santas, and no political or any other kind of statement intended or implied. The Santas marched together, ringing bells and raising money for children's charities.

'Done,' she says, using the Afro-pick on the back of Winston's hair. He starts to pull away. 'Karen, I can do my own hair.'

'I'm just going over the back. Oh, and you'll need your galoshes.'

The costume is heavy, and Winston grumbles that he feels like he's weighed down with saddlebags.

'You'll get used to it – you always do. I'll try to be there at the end. I'm sure the press will turn up... Push yourself, get on the six o'clock news. You need to raise your profile, Winston. Do it for Robbie, if you can't do it for yourself.' Karen doesn't look at him as she says this.

The central heating is on maximum setting, and when Winston leaves the Farm, he welcomes the fresh, glacial chill that throws its arms about him and scrapes against his face.

At Trafalgar Square the Santas are their own species. Laughter and merriment in their vivid, shouting scarlet. Everywhere he looks and turns, Winston sees himself reflected. A warming glow swells in his chest. This is it, the March of a Thousand Santas.

There are onlookers and well-wishers, camera operators, television reporters and event organisers shouting orders and giving directions. Begun ten years ago, the event has grown in popularity and now attracts thousands of visitors from the UK and abroad. Participants mill around the starting line, marked by a wide red banner. Winston approaches the registration tables.

'Winston Booth,' he says.

Bald head down, the man at the desk says nothing but glances at his laptop, scribbles on a form and places a tick beside Winston's name.

'Booth. Winston... 896.'

He hands a sticker to Winston. Not 1000 or even 999 but 896. He feels as if he's going down and the numbers are marking his descent.

The snow's stopped falling and the air is arctic cool and crisp. The route is the same as last year's, travelling through the heart of the city. Down Charing Cross Road, left turn into Oxford Street, then into Regent Street, through Piccadilly Circus, up the Haymarket, left into Pall Mall East and then back to Trafalgar Square and the finishing line. There'll be partying until the early hours with sound systems pumping music and stalls selling chestnuts, hog roast, mince pies, roasted turkey legs, mulled wine and beer. Winston catches sight of regulars he's met in previous years.

Strolling towards Landseer's lions, he notices a short, squat Santa blowing puffs of smoke and staring in his direction. The Santa walks over and stands beside him.

'Freezing, innit?' the smoking Santa says. Lifting her bushy fake beard and curly moustache, she grins.

'Ha. Your face!' she says. 'I'm taking my husband's place this year.'

Winston nods and kicks snow from his shoes. 'That's great, we still don't get enough women Santas.'

'I know, sexist, innit?' she says, pushing long, dark hair under a faux fur-trimmed hood.

Whistles start blowing and there's clapping and cheering as a short, stocky man wearing a thick sheepskin jacket holds a megaphone to his mouth, blows a whistle and booms, 'They're off!'

As they march along Charing Cross Road towards Oxford Street, they pass crowds of smiling, flag-bearing people. Shop assistants stand outside shops to wave them on and bystanders take photos on their phones. Shrill bagpipe notes strike the air with 'The Little Drummer Boy'. The moving forest of Santas generates its own heat and they warm one another as they trudge forward.

'I'm not the only woman doing this, but maybe the only woman taking her husband's place,' she says, walking three steps to each of Winston's long strides.

'Did you register online?'

She shakes her head. 'Nah, didn't bother, I've just signed up now. Had a lot on, what with this and that.'

She looks down.

'I'm sure your husband would be proud of what you're doing.'

'Hope so.'

Winston stifles a cough. 'I'm sure he'd tell you if he could. I know how hard it is when you lose someone.'

She laughs out loud.

'No, my husband's not dead, he's inside. Doing time. Armed robbery.'

'Ah, right. I see.' He doesn't want to pass judgement and tries to look understanding.

The woman sighs. 'We used to argue about how long pasta keeps and there he was planning bank robberies. I had no idea. I knew he had a past and that he was no angel – but armed robbery, Hatton Garden, sawn-off shotguns. It all came as a bit of a blow. We had the press at the door. It was a total nightmare.'

'Life, huh?' Winston says. 'Doesn't always make sense, isn't always fair. You from London?'

'Yep. North London, Haringey.'

'Me too.' He turns to her. 'Whereabouts?'

'Tottenham.'

'Snap.'

There is something familiar about her voice, her cackling laughter – but he's not sure.

'I'm Winston.'

'Penny.'

He thinks hard, looks back but doesn't remember meeting a Penny.

'It was tough at first,' she says. 'Just me on my own with my son. But then it got easier. Ray lives in Germany.'

'Ray?'

'Yeah, my son. He'll be twenty-six next month... You got kids?'

He takes a long time to answer. His eyes scan the faces in the crowd: parents lifting small children so they can sit on the tops of metal barriers, children's faces brimming with giggles, flags held in their little hands.

'No. No kids.'

She nods.

'I was a single mum before I met my husband, Terry. Up the duff at sixteen. Terry wasn't Ray's dad, but he did his best.'

Penny's perfume swathes about him like a silk wrap. A burning, smoky scent. It reminds him of the girls of his youth; pliable, nubile girls. Their smooth, tender skin, the heat of slow-dancing to soul and reggae rhythms at nightclubs like The Royal, Dougie's Hideaway, The Shady Grove Club and The Fridge and coming home plastered, half asleep at work the next day. Winston conquered and trampled hearts, leaving a winding track of emotional debris like a forgotten paper trail.

Karen was from Pinner; back then north-west London was posh. She smelled of Chanel Number Five, wore classy, flat-heeled court shoes and a string of fake pearls around her dainty, slender neck. In the early days, he moved around her like a waiter. He remembers his friends taunting him, calling him a sell-out. His best friend Karl said, 'You can't be black if you sleep white.' Winston told Karl to back off, argued that he knew who he was and what he was regardless of who he dated or slept with. 'It doesn't come off on the sheets, Karl. I'll still be black in the morning.'

He considered posh Karen to be a step up at the time, but now he wonders what happened to the Sharons, Ritas and Paulines of the world, the young women he left behind.

He is jolted back to the present when Penny slips and nearly falls to the ground. He catches her, easing her up with a sure grip.

'You okay?' he asks.

'Yep, but nearly wasn't. Can I hold your arm?'

She loops her arm through his, her hand a comforting, cosy presence. Beside his large-booted footprints, small triangular heels persist in the snow.

They swap ideas about turkey recipes, best stuffing and worst gravy. Her voice jingles and banter grows easily between them.

'Are you married?' she asks.

'Yes.'

'Good. Good for you. Marriage is a great thing when it works. Human beings aren't meant to be alone. We're social creatures, aren't we? No man is an island and all that.' Winston feels her grip tighten on his arm.

'But I bet you sowed your wild oats when you were younger,' she says, a schoolgirl titter in her voice.

'Well, I wasn't a choirboy.' Winston coughs, drawing his collar up to his throat.

'Heartbreaker, I'd put money on it,' Penny says. He notices her nose is turning red with the cold. 'Ray's dad gave me a dodgy phone number and address so I couldn't trace him when I found out I was pregnant. Thought I saw him once, Ray's dad – just once.' And her voice trails off. The wind picks up, gathering and swirling the snow.

'What's she like then, your wife?'

Winston feels hot and sticky inside his costume. The beard is irritating his chin and he wants to pull the damn thing off.

'She's a good woman. Been married twenty-four years.'

'That's rare these days.'

There's a growing edge to her voice, but perhaps it's only the fierce gust of wind altering his hearing. There's a ripple of cheers and roaring among the Santas.

'Ever been tempted to play away?' Penny asks, and Winston suspects that under her beard there is a grimace flickering lizard-like across her lips.

'Can't say I have.'

'Can you say the same for your wife?' Winston feels the growing pressure pull on his arm.

'I'm sure my wife... Look, I don't think we should be having this conversation. My marriage is my business.'

He stiffens, hoping she'll remove her arm, but Penny holds on and each of his steps is dogged down with her dragging movement.

'Sorry, no offence meant. I'm always putting my foot in my mouth, bull in a china shop, that's me. It's just that you remind me of someone from long ago.'

'Really?' He grits his teeth.

'You look so much like him. Ray's dad, I mean. I tried to find him, like I said. Tried Facebook recently, even went back to our old haunts, asked around but I never found him.'

'I'm sure we've never met before. I would have remembered.'

'Would you?' Penny stops, folds her arms and faces him squarely, hard lines puckering her forehead. 'Why would you remember me? To men like you I was just a number, another notch on your belt, a young girl with a head full of dross.' Layers of sweat and cigarette fumes rise from beneath her perfume, suffocating the minty winter air.

'Isn't that right, Winston?' She threads her arm back through his and tries to move them on, but Winston won't budge.

'No, I think I'm going to head off,' he mumbles, and tries to pull his arm away, but she clings on.

He looks down at his boots which are quickly vanishing beneath a fresh powdering of snow.

'Look, I'm very sorry but we've never met before. I don't know you and you don't know anything about me.' Wrenching his arm free, he runs, leaping over a metal barrier, zigzagging through the crowds and hurrying from Penny's voice, which is carried in the wind as she cries out.

He glances back to see her shrinking figure, her arms waving like she's marooned on shore, her call drowning in the surrounding noise. The Santas continue to spill a long line of running crimson along snow-carpeted streets.

Winston wanders, stopping to gaze at glittery, glitzy window displays; his reflection throws back only shadows. Boarding a northbound Piccadilly line tube, he sits next to a man who is dressed like he has a big city job and whose breath smells of whisky. The man insists on telling him his Christmas wish list – a month in Barbados, a promotion to CEO and a new wife – then staggers off the tube, blurting, 'I should be going to Knightsbridge. I'm going the wrong bloody way. Merry Christmas with bells on!'

At Turnpike Lane, Winston climbs into his silver-grey Nissan and drives home. He doesn't expect Karen to be at their house; he'll be home early. She's normally at the finishing line, ready with a thermos flask and a quick kiss. As he opens the front door, he hears voices coming from the living room. He walks in and finds Karen sitting on the sofa next to a pink-faced, grey-suited white man. The man's hair is a thick blond thatch that covers most of his wide forehead.

'Winston, I didn't expect you,' Karen says and her face mottles. 'I was just about to come and meet you.'

The man quickly stands. 'It's not what you think.'

Winston looks through him and turns away.

'John's an old friend from way back. He was just passing.'

Winston says nothing and walks into the hallway. In the bathroom, he takes off his costume, studies his transformation from yuletide hero to suburban zero. Deep lines crease his face. He can still hear Penny's voice calling, strangled by wind and snow. Feeling light-headed, he clutches the edges of the sink to steady himself, realising he's been out in the cold for too long. His eyes scan the oblong body of the sink, the glint of the arched chrome taps and the small bar of white soap, dry and waiting. The plastic toothbrush stand holds his and Karen's toothbrushes. It has four slots and two are vacant. Winston knows there should be four toothbrushes: one for him, one for Karen, one for Robbie and one for the second child they never had. There were meant to be four of them, four of them living here in this house, talking, laughing, quarrelling over the bathroom in the morning, hiding presents under the Christmas tree. There should have been four people in this family – why else would the toothbrush stand have four holes?

Space and emptiness grow around him like cane rising.

He hears the front door close and Karen's heavy steps. She pushes open the bathroom door. He thinks how at ease she looked beside the man, and how different she looks now, caught and fluttering in the palm of one hand.

'I'm sorry,' she says, looking down at the tiled floor.

'Did you know people say "sorry" on average twelve times a day?' Winston says, staring into the mirror. The Santa beard and red cap with its pom-pom are gone along with the light in his eyes.

Karen twists the wedding ring on her finger. 'I don't know what else to say, Winston.'

'I'll say it then, shall I? The thing we can't seem to say. We watched our son die together, Karen. You and I watched Robbie die. And we've never let him go, we've never said goodbye. The infinity box means our pain is forever, we've never allowed ourselves to stop hurting, to move forward. There, I've said it for both of us.'

Thoughts turn like windmills in his mind. He stares up at the bathroom ceiling, at the small concealed lights sunken in their sockets. Cracks like vapoured breath fissure the eggshell paint.

'Haven't you got anything to say, Karen? I've just said the thing we need to say, and you're standing there giving nothing back.'

He thinks of rivers that stop flowing. Sludge forms a strange, makeshift land; a putrefying reprieve to ducks and moorhens. He visualises the skeletons of condemned houses ready for demolition, revealing odd, partial staircases leading nowhere. So it is with the edifice of their lives; he and Karen are left standing.

'I'm not good at this, Winston, I never have been.' Karen wipes tears from her face. 'What do you want me to say?'

'I don't know, something. Anything.'

She swallows hard. 'Anything?'

'Yes, anything.'

She wrings her fingers and says, 'I can't do this. I can't talk about Robbie. I'm sorry but I can't.'

Closing the bathroom door, she walks into the bedroom. Winston continues to look up at the cracks in the ceiling. They're getting worse; they're going to need filling. He hears Karen crying, blowing her nose, and imagines her holding herself, rocking slowly on the edge of the bed, alone in the darkness – but he isn't listening anymore. Winston has nothing left to lose. He hears something different altogether.

VI

Mavis's Story

Most nights Mavis lies awake turning over her life. She longs for sleep like some people pray for rain but sleep doesn't come, not one drop. Corners of her life won't meet and there are gaping bits that she has either neglected or missed. In the morning her feet land on a cold floor and search for worn slippers. She has new slippers somewhere but these ones have taken the shape of her flat feet and cling like thick outer skin. The morning mirror reminds her that she has the sort of face that can't take crying; her small eyes sink back into their sockets. Breakfast is two slices of wholemeal toast, a bowl of cornflakes and a cup of weak tea. Sitting at the dining table, she looks out through the French windows. A glistening white blanket covers the skeletal shrubs and balding grass of her back garden. The snowy eiderdown gives off a piercing radiance, forcing Mavis to look away. She finishes her tea.

Munchies café, where she works, is on Tottenham High Road, between the Halifax bank and what used to be the Daisy Fresh Dry Cleaners. Munchies seats up to fifty diners. Dark plastic-backed chairs are grouped in sets of four around wooden tables, and menus offering every combination of fried breakfast are slipped between bottles of ketchup and vinegar. Thin lines of condensation drizzle down the large windows, but Max, the owner, isn't bothered as long as the café's busy.

Donna has called in sick so Mavis has to pick up her shift. Munchies provides a broad view of Tottenham High Road, looking out onto traffic lights, mums, babies and buggies. The morning moves slowly and only a meagre number of customers brave the cold. Mavis drags the mop's head across the red tiles by the entrance door and covers this with a large sheet of cardboard for customers to step on with their slushy boots and shoes. She has a strange sense that her movements are being studied, and under this scrutiny her usual routine becomes awkward and stilted.

Carrying the mop and bucket through the café, past the cash desk, along the narrow corridor, beyond the kitchen and toilets and out to the backyard, Mavis stacks them by the wall. Her fingers are frozen, numbed by icy air. She's wearing black trousers, a black jumper and a frilly white apron that Max has insisted gives the café 'style'. She fiddles in her pocket for a cigarette, but decides against smoking because it will only set her thinking and she would rather not think. She walks towards table one where the man who has been watching her turns his head from the menu and looks up, smiling.

'It's Maxine, isn't it?' he asks.

Her name has been Mavis for forty-five years. Mavis Margaret Browne with a life missed.

'Yes, Maxine,' Mavis hears herself replying, not wanting to disappoint. The man's smile broadens and a jig sets up a rhythm in Mavis's chest.

Her elderly mother died two years ago, after breaking off Mavis's engagement with life. By continually complaining of illness she had pruned her daughter's role in life to full-time nurse. At carers' meetings Mavis listened closely as Mr Norris, Barbara Braystar and Cupcake shared their stories of love and devotion, often in tears. Mavis cried too, but for different reasons. Her tears fell because she had never felt such love and suspected she never would.

Mavis had given up on men and relationships, and after her mother's death, she felt like a spat-out pip. With blood boiling in her veins, she dug up her mother's beloved blue hydrangeas. She had always hated their bitter, industrial smell. She tossed the plants into a green recycling bag and dumped it in the front garden for rubbish collection. Two years later there is very little on which she pegs her life apart from working in Munchies and the routine of housekeeping and shopping.

'So how are you doing?' the man asks.

Mavis nods. 'I'm good.'

'Still with the choir then? I heard the conductor was a bit of a diva, but he had a heart of gold by all accounts. You were great though, you all were. How's your daughter?'

Mavis had wanted children. A son. A daughter. Keen-eyed kids, excited steps running up and down the stairs. Sticky hands squeezing nuggets of Lego; lost and found.

'Yes, she's fine.'

'At uni now, I expect?'

Mavis's daughter would have wanted to change the world.

'Yes, she's studying Politics.'

'You don't look old enough to have a daughter that age,' he says. Mavis hears a lower, softer note in his voice, sees his eyes take in her face with a different interest.

'What can I get you?' Mavis asks, fiddling with her notepad.

'Full English.'

As she returns to the kitchen, Mavis feels the man's curiosity travel down the length of her back. She hands the chef the order and he drives the paper slip through one of the small metal stakes where orders for food grow. Through the rectangular slit at the top of the door, she studies the man seated at table one. He's reading one of the tabloids they keep lying around. She notes his even features and the heavy flop of dark hair. He does a jerky thing with his shoulders as if he's clearing his throat with his whole body and is about to apologise or break some bad news.

'This looks good,' he beams as Mavis places the sizzling plate before him. 'I'm starving. I've never been much of a cook and since the divorce – well, you know how it is.' She doesn't. Her fingers tense inside her pockets.

'Yes,' she says, 'divorce is never easy.'

After her mother broke her ankles in a fall, the old woman became increasingly obstinate, refusing bed baths and regularly overturning plates of food and bowls of soup. A serious respiratory infection shortly before her death reduced her to a bedbound bundle of breathlessness and wheezing. Dr Lewis, the family doctor, advised Mavis to prepare herself and she did, with a quiet, guilty unbuttoning. In the morning, she bent over her mother's face and, bringing her head down, listened carefully but she wasn't sure if the old woman was still breathing. There was a frozen stillness in the room, all around them an observant clamminess. Her mother's face was pinched, scaled down; her eyes closed, her mouth a dark crevice. Mavis panicked. Grabbing a pillow, she held it down over her mother's face, while she looked away, her eyes focused on the faded wallpaper pattern of rambling roses and wilting trellis.

'It's for the best, Mother, for you and me,' Mavis whispered, pinning the pillow down with all her force.

Dr Lewis concluded that the old woman had died in the early hours of the morning; Mavis told him that she had found her that way. Patting her shoulder, Dr Lewis said, 'Went in her sleep. Best way. Your mum is at peace now, you've done all you can.'

Murder is murder, thought Mavis, whether by inched degree or in one guillotined swoop – but mercy killing is a kindness. A kindness her mother hadn't deserved.

'You on your own then?' the man asks.

Mavis nods.

She has never been anything else. An only child; tea parties with Big Ted and Freckles Bailey, her rag doll. At primary school, Mavis had one friend who was older than her but behaved like a much younger child. Her name was Solbeth Murray. Small, slight, toffee-coloured Solbeth. Other kids used to call Solbeth half-caste; for them she was too black to be white and too white to be black.

Once, slow-walking along Black Boy Lane, Solbeth turned to Mavis and said, 'I hate it when Shirley and Susan call me half-caste. I ain't half anything. Nothing's missing, I'm all here. Mum and Dad say it's Shirley and Susan that's got the bits missing.' They kind-of laughed, chewing Curly Wurlys, linking arms, careful not to step on pavement cracks and break their mothers' backs.

At secondary school, Mavis was relegated to backing-group status while starlets like Angela Bliss and Sophie Eddy took centre stage. Angela and Sophie were the first to be kissed, dated, romanced, engaged, married and impregnated, and not necessarily in that order. Once Mavis saw Angela Bliss pop into Munchies for a takeaway, or at least she thought she recognised the extravagant, floaty hair and quickly found a reason to do a stock check out back.

Many years ago, Mavis danced with a man who didn't ask her name. Afterwards they left the Maze nightclub for a hurried fumble. She remembers the furnace of his single bed and how his blunt fingers probed between her legs. She felt like she was biting into ice, jarring and exhilarating all at once. When it was over, he rolled to the side and took all the duvet with him. Each time he exhaled he whistled and once he cried out in words Mavis didn't understand. When he woke in the morning, he fried eggs and thick slices of white bread.

'You need husband,' he said with a thick Albanian accent. Unsure whether this was a question or an observation, Mavis smiled. She was her mother's daughter and her mother had pronounced, 'With a chin like that you'll never amount to anything.' Men's lives ran parallel to her own; they seldom entered her world or crossed her path.

Her father died when she was very young. He had been a grey, fleeting figure who treated the Bellamy Furniture Company, where he was a foreman, as a second home, surrounded by upholstery and machinery. Mavis's memories of him are scant. Her mother didn't believe in keeping photographs, seeing little point in what she called 'a continual raking up of the past'.

The man puts down his knife and fork and does the jerky thing.

'How about you and me meeting up? I'd love to take you out. God, you must think I'm pushy.'

Mavis shakes her head. 'No, you're not being pushy. I'd like that.'

His name is Steve Holloway. Area Manager for the local Somerfield supermarket.

On Friday morning Mavis tries on a beige dress she's had for years and keeps in the back of the wardrobe. Donna would have given her advice but she's been off work with the flu and Mavis isn't able to contact her. Studying her reflection in the full-length wardrobe mirror, she turns her head from side to side, frowning. She isn't sure how the dress should fit, but it sags about her body. After work Mavis decides to buy a black dress that fits closely around her broad frame. The shop assistant eggs her on, twittering about curves and flaunting, not knowing that Mavis's body has long been left fallow.

In the evening, Steve Holloway collects Mavis from her large detached house on the corner of Sperling Road and The Avenue. He takes her to Valentino's, a new restaurant near Enfield town centre. It is described as serving fine Italian cuisine.

Inside, the restaurant is spacious and brightly lit: framed photographs of Robert De Niro, Sophia Loren and brooding Mafia men in gangster uniforms cover the walls. There are tan leather chairs around each table and pale-cream fake marble columns dotted throughout.

A waiter shows them to their table. Smiling, he places a linen napkin on her lap and calls Mavis *signora*. She orders *pasta e fagioli* and is very careful not to slurp. She concentrates on her breathing while listening to Steve talk about his work, his divorce, his house that needs a new roof and his 'minted' brother who lives in Grand Cayman. The conversation turns to vermin; mice, rats and foxes.

'But I can't see them as vermin,' Mavis says. 'I like foxes. They're always scampering around my back garden and I don't mind.'

'Really?'

'Oh yes, a whole family stayed behind the garden shed not long ago.'

'Well, foxes are vermin in my book, along with rats, pigeons and Canada geese. They're very clever, I'll give you that. Cunning. Ripping open bin liners, always on the lookout.'

Again she notices the odd habit Steve has of jerking his shoulders as if something has snagged in the back of his jacket. He continues talking about all the things he hates, and Mavis watches as he tears the tender chicken wings. She likes his hands; capable, focused hands with long piano fingers. Sometimes she veers off from what he says and then hones in again when his voice grows quiet.

'You don't talk much, do you?' Steve says. She shakes her head, considering the real Maxine and the possibility of discovery. Never fraudulent before, she senses her life has been an imitation of a life lived. On her doorstep, she enjoys the soft pressure of his lips and forgets the cool precision of his fingers peeling skin from chicken wings.

The sex is a kind of taking off but Mavis never stops observing her body moving, touching and being touched. She believes she can't give over, so when her body opens up and something molten rushes inside, she hides her tearful gratitude and whispered sorrys in the bones of his shoulders.

Cinema, dinners, talk, touching, sex. She likes the way Steve moves her body, taking charge. As if opening a can, he hooks the ring and tugs; Mavis welcomes the new, unlidded exposure. Counting the moles she's always disliked, Steve calls them beauty spots and kisses number eight. She has always believed her body simple and box-like but he introduces her to delicate tiers and layers. Sexing her, Steve Holloway brings back the wonder of cartwheels she turned as a child. She lies awake one night, her eyes studying the light cast by the lamp post outside. It hits the ceiling with one long diagonal stroke and creates a sloping white bar across the bed, illuminating her right foot and left thigh. She waits for the night when the moonlight breaks through the blinds and sinks their spent bodies in a mercury pool.

Mavis now stands with her feet confidently rooted on the ground. She wears poppy-red lipstick and discovers plunging necklines. To hell with the neighbours and the fortunes of black bin liners; she leaves morsels of meat for her brazen new friends, the foxes.

'I wouldn't go encouraging them,' Steve warns but Mavis ignores him.

One busy lunchtime, four grey-suited men take seats at table six. They don't look at Mavis when they give their orders: a round of lattes and toasted ham and egg sandwiches.

Too big for the smallish chairs, the men look out of place, and she wants to shoo them out to the nearest Starbucks so that she can make way for the café's regular, deserving customers – locals, loose-footed loners, lorry drivers and those from the Farm or the Job Centre. Carrying the coffees and sandwiches on a dark metal tray, she walks towards table six.

'He's only gone and got himself a bit on the side,' one of the men says, pulling at his tie as Mavis places the mugs and plates on the table.

'He told me she's a lonely old bird. Ugly as sin. Big house, all paid off. Made out he's known her for years. Lying git. She's given him money, bought him fancy presents. He said he's fallen on hard times, going through a nightmare divorce. Dozy cow's been taken in. Hook, line and sinker... I don't know how Holloway does it.'

Their shoulders make a wall that breaks apart with laughter. The metal tray falls to the floor and, with mumbled apologies, Mavis quickly wipes up the spill.

She tells Max she feels ill. She can't remember removing her apron, changing her shoes, putting on her coat or leaving the café.

When Mavis arrives home, she shuts the front door; for once she doesn't yearn for the outside world. Without removing her coat, she walks into the dining room and sits by the table. The old house is cold and dark. She hasn't bothered with redecoration or refurbishment, and the house remains as it was when she was a child.

Sitting in the dark, listening to something breathing in the heavy silence, Mavis hears her mother's voice:

'You're a silly goose, Mavis, always were. He saw you coming... You're a Plain Jane, you take after your father's side of the family. Take an honest look in the mirror, then ask yourself what a man like that is doing with a woman like you.'

Into the dark, Mavis replies, 'Hush, Mother.'

Weary with thought, she walks upstairs. Velveteen drapes, an old maplewood dressing table with a speckled glass mirror and a shabby wicker ottoman at the foot of her bed. Everything is still in its place and she wonders why she expected anything to have changed. It is no longer just her bedroom. She remembers the meetings of bodies and the smooth outline of her shape that Steve Holloway drew with his deft fingers. She allows her hands to touch the ribbed candlewick spread.

On the bed, Mavis curls into a tight ball.

'Oh, what a tangled web we weave, when first we practise to deceive.'

'Be quiet, Mother.'

The house swells around her and Mavis succumbs to its shelter. Walls rise up like hedges and she's reminded of the safety found in the pillowed peat of shadows.

The phone rings at eight o'clock, nine o'clock and again at ten o'clock. It remains unanswered. She reaches for the television remote and increases the volume. In the days that follow, letters, not texts, arrive. One each week. Noting the curls and loops in the sprawling handwriting, Mavis realises that Steve is thinking on paper.

Behind the words, she visualises the strong grasp of his hand, the bend of his arm as he writes. In margins he scribbles funny faces and doodles love-hearts. Beginning with confusion, he writes that he doesn't understand why she hasn't been in touch. He details his heartbreak and grief. After these first messages come long, sinuous letters of apology and shame. He says he wants to be honest, to put the record straight; he admits that he hasn't been going through a divorce, there isn't a 'minted' brother, that he has lied. In spiralling letters, he offers explanations about being a dropout, getting on the wrong side of the law, having a drunken, wayward father, a sad, tethered mother, making bad choices.

When Mavis replies and agrees to meet him after his constant pleading, Steve Holloway doesn't write back. The letters stop coming and she realises she now knows too much. Late one evening, she drags a rickety chair from the kitchen into the garden and settles it as steadily as she can in the middle of the lawn. Tilting her head back, she drinks from a bottle of Pinot Noir as she tosses Steve's letters one by one into a metal-mesh fire basket where she regularly incinerates lifeless and decaying things. As the silent night deepens, she watches all her longings go up in flames.

Months later, over breakfast Mavis reads about a local woman who has refused to turn her clocks back during autumn. The woman complains about being robbed of daylight, about having had enough of the gloom. With a growing Facebook following she has sparked a quiet revolution. Mavis wonders how she arranges appointments, meetings, time. When a doctor's receptionist says three o'clock, the woman must translate this to two o'clock, old time, like when decimalisation was first introduced and people used to convert new money into old money and back again. In the article, the woman is quoted as saying she has been seriously ill but the illness has gifted her with a new way of seeing.

Her name is Gladys Pringle and her book is entitled *Saving Time*. Mavis has ordered it online. People say Gladys is living on borrowed time; Mavis isn't sure what this means, but wishes she knew her. The story reminds her of when she was a child and tried to stare down the sun but afterwards needed glasses. Life continued pushing her back each time she tried to rise up against it or asked a different question.

Standing on her patch of lawn, Mavis looks down at her wellingtons and wonders whether there is a small bone of courage somewhere in her body plotting a bold and candid revolution. Possibilities of cruises and Salsa lessons with Max, the owner of Munchies, come to mind – he's asked her often enough.

Dismissing the broken-down fence and the lean-to garden shed, she remembers the bright meadow of blooms that will make a festival of the flower beds in spring.

Colours and scents will blend and dance like crazy without the slur of her mother's hydrangeas. Clearing dead leaves and broken branches, Mavis decides that when spring arrives she'll begin by cutting away those confusing flowers that resemble weeds and rooting out the weeds that hide between the shrubs, slyly pretending to be flowers.

VII

Norma's Story

Through the net curtains of her living room window, Norma Norris looks out at Mount Pleasant Road. She likes watching the kids from the Farm on their skateboards. They sometimes skate outside and in the Lordship Skatepark. She listens to them laugh and talk about their tricks; kickflips, pops and tailslides. She even knows some of their names – Ricky, Kevin. Her focus suddenly shifts as the woman who lives on the opposite side of the road rushes past, a lacy black slip hanging below the hem of her skirt. Norma sighs. She wants the woman's high heels and the places they take her – shoes that would stiletto Norma out of her monotonous life. With heavy, plodding steps Norma's husband Frank walks into the living room.

'All right, then?' he asks.

'All right, then?' Norma mimics in her head and turns away. Silly sod.

'Oh, like that is it?' he says, raising his eyebrows and scratching his head.

The gaoler and the gaoled. He thinks he can detect and read her every mood and emotion, and Norma wants to shout that he can't. She doesn't need a mouthpiece. Words wearing heavy duty boots clump around her head, but she can't wear or use them.

In the early hours of the morning, words wake Norma, calling her to attention. She has worked out that because she can no longer talk, people think she needs their words to do her thinking, feeling and speaking for her. She remembers the timid shadow of a woman she was before the stroke; before the cruel lightning that stole her voice and all movement and sensation on the right side of her body.

Like most people, she had assumed that her ability to speak would always be with her, like her pearly fingernails or the wiry texture of her light-brown hair.

If Norma had known her voice would be robbed from her shortly before her fortieth birthday, she wouldn't have been the compliant, much-too-quiet and docile fool she had been. She would have shouted from rooftops and roared from pulpits. She is convinced God takes away those gifts we don't use. Norma equates her earlier silence and saintly forbearance with a sentimental notion of saving pennies in this life for the life hereafter, as if she could cash in her humility once she got to 'the other side'. Gratefully and fearfully, she nibbled humble pie for most of her life, and she isn't surprised that her husband now believes he can think, feel and speak for her. He tells other people what Norma wants for her birthday, what supper she prefers, what outfits she feels comfortable in and when she's feeling depressed.

'Not in a good mood today then, eh?' Frank says. 'Feeling a bit low, are we?'

Norma's annoyance dissolves when she considers Frank's own need to manage the skewed situation in which they now find themselves. For many years before the stroke, Norma's life had ticked on with neither shock nor surprise. She'd always been the 'grin-and-bear-it, mustn't-grumble' kind. Her doting father had called her a lamb; a gentle little lamb. Never any trouble. Norma had been a dutiful wife. Summer after summer, Christmas pudding after Christmas pudding with no change. And then, one random autumn afternoon, part of her brain suffered a sudden death. Her life is now split into two chapters: before the stroke and after the stroke. The time before the stroke grows dimmer and thinner, as if viewed through a long, narrowing funnel. Norma's face was pleasant enough before the fall. Nothing spectacular. Always a quiet, quick touch of napkin here, with practised precision, to either side of her mouth. No seconds, no extras, no gluttony, no indulgence. Manners before a fall. Always.

The right side of Norma's face falls like a stage curtain, dragged down by a cruel twist so that she's unable to smile and looks at the world with a partial scowl. Inwardly she repeats to herself that she is not a victim, she has dreams and a will of her own.

Her husband works part-time as a manager at Tottenham's McKinnon Brewing Company. Frank brushes Norma's hair so that it hides the right side of her face and tells her she prefers it that way. Once, with a violent and sudden movement, she tugged her hair back with her left hand.

'But we're going to Linda's wedding. I thought you'd...' he began.

No, this is what you want, not what I want, thought Norma. I am still here, still in here, in this body, in this brain, she wanted to scream. Frank hovered over her, seeming unsure as to where to put his hands. Probably around my neck, Norma suspects.

All this from a man who, on alternate Thursday nights, finds the courage to make love to her with his face turned away, looking towards the bedroom window. He mumbles

'Forgive me' afterwards and mops her up, just like he wipes Norma's mouth after she's finished eating. His mess, her mess, their mess. Norma is as much Frank's gaoler as he is hers; the key passes between them, to and fro.

The speech therapist, Miss Perkins, tries to encourage her to speak, to dig up whatever shrunken croak of voice survives but the sound of it, hoarse and alien, repulses Norma.

'Come on, Mrs Norris, you must try harder,' Miss Perkins coaxes. 'A stroke is always a shock, but we'll work on it – perseverance is the order of the day.'

Norma wants to tell pretty Miss Perkins to piss off; Miss Perkins who speaks in clear, clipped tones between moist, generous lips. She's manicured and pedicured, with the kind of hair that swishes. Only the best lovemaking for her, Norma thinks. Cum upon cum upon cum. Norma refuses to sound letters and won't play. At the end of the session, Frank shakes his head and apologises to Miss Perkins on Norma's behalf. He thanks her for her dedication and patience, and Norma catches his eyes caressing Miss Perkins's long, shapely legs. He finds his grip on Norma's wheelchair, and they begin their lonely trek home.

It's a tragedy, people say. What a terrible, terrible thing to have happened – and to such good people. Norma Norris is an inspiration, a wonderful person who gives to charities and supports the March of a Thousand Santas. All this going on about her goodness from well-meaning others, over and over, their unending sympathy. She's left silent, storing the tragedy and sympathy in her body.

A small orange notebook and blue biro are tied to Norma's wheelchair. They hang on short strings and she's encouraged to write. Being right-handed means she can't grasp the pen in her left hand well enough to form whole words, but occasionally she attempts a Y or N. Frank mentions buying 'mood faces'.

'Miss Perkins told me about them – they sell them in Smiths. There's a face for every feeling,' Frank says. 'All you've got to do is point.'

Norma pulls at her biro and scrawls a large 'N', refusing to be riddled or defined.

Determined to throw off the mantle of broken, dependent woman, Norma secretly learns to walk a few steps. Once, Frank leaves her by the living room window, which he tells her is her favourite spot. On his return he finds her gone. Racing around the house, he darts from room to room until he finds her sitting on their bed.

'How?' he blabbers, his arms wide.

Very slowly and weakly, Norma stands.

'How long...? How long?!' he shouts.

Turning away, he mutters something that she can't hear; rough words, she knows, clamped between his lips.

'Don't go pushing yourself,' Frank says. 'We have to accept things as they are. We mustn't make things worse.'

Norma realises Frank has been secretly sucking on her disability like forbidden fruit when he thinks no one is watching. She once heard of a man who had walked on crutches for most of his life, only to be cured during a church healing service. A fortnight later, the man attacked the preacher who had healed him, stabbing him forty-three times with a bread knife and complaining that the preacher had stolen his reason for staying alive. Norma believes people need crutches. On Thursday night, Frank giggles, calls her a 'very naughty girl' and, flipping her over, buries her face in the pillow.

Dr Abimbola, the family doctor, marvels at Norma's progress. With a smile that dimples her well-padded, round face, she says, 'Mrs Norris, you are a miracle woman.' Swiftly Norma passes from tragic to miraculous; there is no normality, no solace to be found anywhere. No air pocket through which she might breathe.

In the evening, sitting in the armchair nearest the radiator, Frank soaks his feet in a plastic bowl filled with blue Radox and hot water.

'They're killing me,' he groans and rubs at his heels. 'Gout in my big toe, Dr Abimbola says. Can you believe it? There, right under the skin.' He shakes his head. 'What next?'

He massages his ankles. Norma recognises the pain that marks his face, but would swap her wheelchair for his gout in an instant. She wonders how the hard crystals beneath Frank's skin got there, if the tiny particles of gout crept in while he slept, conspiring to find a bridge into his body; do the crystals have a life and intent of their own? And why a big toe? For Norma bodies are mysteries. They commit mutiny every day but are never held to account.

Frank hires Moira Brosnan to assist with caring for Norma and to help around the house. She's a lanky woman with meaty pink arms. Moira's bawdy jokes kick the sombre mood of the house to the kerb, defying anyone to mope or skulk. Even her buttercup-patterned overalls shout 'sunshine'. Norma thinks that Moira reserves a special voice for her as if speaking to her through a magical vessel or along a maze wall, and when it's time to put her feet up, Moira is at her best.

'Well, Norma love, it's time for my little break.'

She lights a cigarette and fans away the smoke.

'Frank says you won't mind me smoking and I hope you don't.'

It is this quality of Moira's that Norma values most, the recognition of another interpretation, the possibility of an alternative view, the acknowledgment she might sometimes get it wrong.

'Coffee's cold,' Moira mutters. 'Nothing quite as nasty as cold coffee, eh, Norma, love? Are you still looking through that window? I caught a glimpse of Ms Braystar earlier. Very glamorous.'

Norma wants to smile and share her observations and thoughts. Yes, she's seen Ms Braystar.

'I went to school with her dad, you know, fancied him something rotten. Rob Braystar. He was drop-dead gorgeous. Looked like a young Antonio Banderas. That's where Ms Braystar gets her good looks, not her mother. Lola Slack had nothing to her but a scrunched-up face full of pimples.'

Then there it is, the deep, throaty chuckle, like cold milk crackling through Rice Krispies. Norma loves Moira's laugh; it makes her feel warm inside. After she plonks her coffee cup on the dining table, Moira smoothes the white tablecloth with sweeping hand-strokes.

'Well, if Barbara Braystar wants to live a particular lifestyle, that's her business. Can't be easy bringing up her little boy on her own. He was born like that, you know. So his mum lap dances, does a trick here and there, so what? We all do what we have to do to get by. It is what it is.' Moira becomes quiet and still. For a moment she seems to disappear and rise somewhere else.

'I can't stomach those precious, holier-than-thou types,' she continues, a frown folding her face. 'Yunno, the ones who judge everyone else and bang on about Tottenham going to the dogs. We're all right, Tottenham's all right. At least with the likes of Barbara Braystar you know where you are. And our neighbourhood will never be monotone or dreary. Always glorious Technicolor. Glorious Technicolor Tottenham.'

Moira chuckles and slides her feet into bright yellow Crocs.

'Something else, Norma, love,' Moira says softly, along the maze wall. 'Believe it or not, you're part of the local colour, too. You're a legend, Norma Norris.'

Stubbing out her cigarette in a small glass ashtray, Moira walks to the kitchen, from where Norma hears the sound of water running and crockery being moved.

A legend. Looking through the net curtains, a small tear runs down Norma's face. She spots Frank heading home, scurrying along the road. His key turns in the lock and she takes a heavy breath, her mask in place.

'Afternoon, Moira,' Frank says. 'I just signed for a package for Warren next door. Postman said there was no reply. I've leant the box against the wall in the hallway. They'll probably call for it later. Not sure what they're up to – he seems to be landscaping the garden or something.'

Moira mumbles in reply.

'How's she been?' Frank asks. Norma guesses he's nodded over in her direction as he hangs up his coat.

'Who knows, Frank? We can only guess. Only our Norma knows that.'

'Huh? Oh, yes. Yes, of course,' he says, and then in a quieter voice adds, 'Moira, I've a little favour to ask of you.'

Norma listens closely.

'Something important?' Moira asks.

'The thing is, I need to be somewhere else this coming Saturday. It's an away-day for carers. Group support. Someone has to take care of the carers,' he says.

'Yes, of course,' she says.

'Could you look after Norma? I'll be leaving at about 9am.'

'When will you be back?'

'Well, that's a tricky one,' Frank says. 'These things have a way of running on. I might stay over.' Norma imagines Frank doing that thing he does when he's nervous, running his little finger along the inside of his shirt collar and toying with his top button.

'Will you be able to help?' he asks Moira.

'Of course. No problem, Mr Norris.'

'Good. There'll be double rates, of course. Oh, and I'd be grateful if you could keep this under your hat. We don't want anyone on the road getting the wrong end of the stick and thinking I'm neglecting old Norma.'

Old Norma.

'Of course, Mr Norris. There's enough gossip on this single street alone to keep tongues wagging for a month of Sundays. Mind you, it's not just Mount Pleasant Road – people everywhere just love gossip and spreading stories, especially juicy ones.'

'Yes, quite,' he says.

Steps sound along the hallway until Frank pushes open the living-room door. Striding into the middle of the room, he asks Norma, 'Feeling peckish? Fancy a bit of grub?'

She hates the word 'grub', and no, she isn't hungry. She's full, hates being waited on; she reads resentment in her husband's eyes. Norma, the lonely legend. No sunset. No boulevard.

'Right then,' Frank says in a voice she knows is meant to chivvy them along.

He returns with a plate of fish and chips and a bib.

'There,' he says, adjusting the bib.

Moira knocks at the door.

'Well, I'll be off, then, Mr and Mrs N. Now, Mrs Norris, you take care of yourself and don't you forget your dreams,' she winks.

Norma wants to wink, smile and cry all at the same time.

'And Saturday?' Frank says.

Moira nods, but remains standing. She stares hard at Frank, who clears his throat and turns to Norma.

'Norma, dear, I'm going to a carers' meeting on Saturday. It's our annual away-day – routine stuff, you know – and Moira has very kindly offered to take care of you. You get on well with Moira, don't you? Of course you do,' he says. 'Good girl.' He pats Norma on the knee. She feels like Buffy, her late mother's Labrador, who had to be put down.

'Well, Moira, that seems to be that,' Frank says. 'All sorted. We'll see you on Saturday, then.'

Norma studies Frank's face while he feeds her, cold metal against her tongue. The spoon frequently misses her mouth and meets her chin or her teeth. She would kick him if she could. The whole procedure takes place in silence and as Norma stares at him, she notes the heavy, sagging skin padding his doughy face. He is clean-shaven, but the boyishness that years ago attracted her now seems wrongly pudgy and pubescent.

Carers' meeting. Carers' meeting. Norma has smelled the carer's perfume and heard her scuttling steps on the front-garden path. From the window she has seen the secret smiles and waves exchanged. There are phone calls made in the dark den of night when Norma pretends to be asleep. Calls made to the other carer who lives across the road, Barbara Braystar. Norma has heard Frank call her Babs darling. Hot lips. My love. Sweetheart. Goddess. Heard him whisper that he 'can't wait'. All that caring, all that loving. Norma wants to congratulate him, to say she understands, knows about the thirst and the need for air pockets.

Saturday arrives and Frank is awake at 6am. He dresses Norma in a dark-green belted crimplene dress.

'There,' he says, positioning Norma in her wheelchair by the window. He hums and tiny drops of perspiration pepper his upper lip.

Norma thinks he's left the house, but when she turns she finds him scuttering about in the living room. She realises that in reality Frank left years ago. Moira arrives promptly and dressed in a flimsy, creamy blouse and smart black trousers. Norma's only ever seen her dressed for work.

'All right, then, I'll be going. See you first thing tomorrow morning,' Frank says, without looking back. 'Thank you, Moira.'

Norma watches Frank hurry down the path towards all that caring. Perfumed arms and perfumed legs wait to wrap themselves around him. Limbs, wings, the same thing.

Moira sits on the sofa, slips off her flats and fluffs up her fine curly hair.

'Now, Norma, my love, are you up for a day of fun?'

Moira glows like a fairy godmother.

'I've been doing a lot of thinking and I suspect you're bored, cooped up in this house. Being stuck in here day after day would drive me mad. But today is your birthday.'

It's not my birthday, Norma thinks.

'Well, we both know it's not really your birthday,' Moira says. 'But how about pretending and having some "unbirthday" treats anyway? You know, like the song the Mad Hatter sings to Alice?'

Moira never stops surprising her. She describes the kind of day Norma dreams about. She dumps the frumpy crimplene frock in the bottom of a linen basket and helps to dress Norma in a pale pink angora top and a floaty black skirt. They spend three hours in the Bodylicious Beauty Salon and have high tea at the nearby White Hart Hotel. Moira glides the wheelchair effortlessly as they whizz along, successfully navigating stairs and cabs, before returning home.

Just after 7pm, the doorbell rings. Moira leads two smartly dressed men into the living room. They drench the air with strong aftershave. One man is tall and dwarfs Moira. The other one is short, his face gaunt and beaky. He smiles at Norma and she scolds herself for being unable to smile back. She watches him shuffle from one foot to the other.

'Stop fidgeting,' Moira says to the short man.

Moira and the men stand before Norma as if on parade, and she wishes she could tell them to sit down.

'This is my Ron.' Moira nudges the taller man in the side. 'My other half.'

Ron smiles. He is a giant and occupies a good-sized chunk of shadow and space.

'And this is Louis,' Moira says, gesturing to the shorter man, who steps forward with a swagger.

'Zasny. Louis Zasny,' he says in a strong New York accent. 'I'm Russian, Miss Norma. Russian by way of Brooklyn, New York. Jewish Russian, that is. I'm a tailor by trade—'

'All right, all right. Norma doesn't need your life history. You're just Lou to us and that's about as good as it gets, okay? Okay. Good. We've got to get a move on.'

Moira explains the mechanics of the wheelchair and Louis Zasny steers Norma along the hallway. In the minicab, Moira explains to Norma that they're going to Chancey's Electric Cabaret in Soho.

The club is tucked away in a dark corner of Sherwood Mews. Norma is wheeled into a subterranean cave where the walls are painted black. They head down a long ramp to a small round table just in front of the stage. Moira, Ron and Lou seem to know a lot of people; nods and waves are swapped. Other wheelchair users sit close to the side of the stage.

'Isn't that Della over there?' Moira asks Ron. 'That holiday seems to have worked wonders.' Norma glances over at a woman with piled-up auburn curls sitting at the opposite table. She's downing a goblet of deep red wine and complaining very loudly about the need for air conditioning. It is warm and Norma wishes she was wearing something lighter.

'Been to a cabaret before, Norma, love?' Moira asks. 'Well, this is cabaret bordering on burlesque.'

'It's the same thing,' Ron says.

'No way,' Lou says. 'Cabaret is classier. It's not just hooters, booty and bubbly. It's not about getting your glitz out and wearing frilly panties for the boys. Hell no. It's more than that. I've seen a lot of comedians get their breaks in cabaret. Bette Midler began in cabaret. Burlesque is a different kit and kaboodle. It's just sleaze, sex. Here we're talking variety – art.'

Moira rolls her eyes. 'Whatever. Let's just have a bloody good time.'

There is an energy and a buzz in the club; people are talking and laughing. Slowly the lights fade. The band strikes up brassy, jazzy sounds and from the ceiling a glistering silver ball starts spinning as the compère walks onto the stage. She is petite and naked but for a few strategically placed feather boas and strips of strobe lighting.

'Welcome, one and all!' the hostess yells. 'Welcome to

Chancey's Electric Cabaret! Tonight we have sights and sounds to thrill, entertain and astound you!'

Norma's eyes are fixed on the stage. The air is smoggy with sweat and hormones; she feels an excitement and a stirring she hasn't felt for a long time.

The first act is the Trucking Texas Sisters. The lead dancer steps forward and in a deep, throaty voice says, 'Well, howdy y'all. We're the Texas Sisters coming all the way from El Paso!' Moira leans over and tells Norma they're from Romford. Densely tattooed from head to toe, they wear Stetson hats and frilly tulle tutus. Twirling and fluttering to melodramatic arias they enact the *Madame Butterfly* death scene and collapse in Swan Lake fashion at the end of their dance. Mock blood covers their hands and stomachs. At least, Norma hopes it's fake.

They end their act with graceful, delicate curtsies, and are quickly followed by a blind Blues singer who introduces himself as Sunny Day. He sits on a stool and holds his guitar like a lover.

'I've heard this guy before,' Lou whispers. 'Pure genius.'

Sunny Day reduces Norma to silent tears as he soulfully sings 'Killing Me Softly'. Next is Kamala. She's a razor-tongued, sari-wearing Asian comedian from Bradford. A fluorescent green bindi marks the centre of her forehead.

'Yo, sisters. Tonight I'm gonna talk about love, sex and marriage.' A big toothy grin slides across her striking golden-brown face.

'I'm telling it like it is, girlfriends, so buckle up, boys.' There are loud hoots and whistles from the audience. 'I've been married three times. My last husband added some much-needed spice to our marriage... Yep, he left. Just as well, he was a terrible liar. How did I know he was lying? His lips were moving. He wasn't even circumcised! Yeah, he was a complete dick! I keep asking myself, if they can send a man to the moon, why can't they send them all? And sisters, don't ever think you can change a man unless he's in nappies!'

The crowd roars with laughter. Norma's head is spinning. A reggae-jazz fusion band, Astral, takes to the stage and people start dancing. Astral are followed by Magic Max, a magician from Croydon in a sequin-studded bowler hat, who does bizarre things with cactus plants, dildos and pickles; they appear from his shirt sleeves and out of his ears and mouth, and at one point Norma looks down because he's about to do something potentially painful to his eyes.

'Ouch,' Lou says.

Norma feels Louis Zasny's eyes studying her face; he reaches over and takes her hand. This little man with tender marcasite eyes makes her feel new. Moira and Ron stroll hand in hand over to the dance floor and join the cluster of smooching, dancing couples moving like one animal in the velvet dark. Louis leans closer and whispers, 'Do you believe that anything is possible?'

Norma burns to the base of her roots and beginnings. She looks away and across at the dancing couples.

'I do,' Louis says. 'We're all more than what we appear to be. We're all dreamers, dancers. And while we're here every single moment counts, Miss Norma. Listen to me going on like an old fool. I know I talk way too much but every nut and bolt is working.' He folds his fist and raps the side of his head. 'No disrespect meant... It's just that sometimes we forget how precious this short piece of glory is.'

Crap, Norma thinks. She hates psychobabble and all that New-Age drivel. He's swallowed too many pop-psychology books.

'All I'm saying is you can dance if you want to.' He squeezes Norma's hand.

She gazes down.

'This jazz ain't just for the Moiras and Rons of the world. It's for Norma and Louis, too.'

When Norma walks a little each day from the living room to the bedroom, she shuffles forward with her left foot and drags her right leg behind her like a plank of wood. He'll have to help her. She looks at Lou for a long time until he stands and begins to lift her up. The weight falls to her feet and her legs turn to marrow. She falls against him, but he holds her.

The music doesn't stop until Norma arrives home after 4am. Moira tucks her in bed while Louis and Ron drink mugs of hot chocolate in the living room.

'I hope you enjoyed tonight,' Moira says. 'Not too risqué, was it? Lou's a decent sort. I used to look after his wife when they lived in Stamford Hill. After his wife died he bought a smaller place, but he still plays pool with Ron every week. I hope you didn't mind him coming along but I bet you wouldn't have enjoyed being a gooseberry. Good show, wasn't it? Hope you had fun. Night, Norma, love.'

Norma closes her eyes and dreams of being centre stage in her wheelchair. Like kids from the Farm on their skateboards, she performs wheelies, figures of eight and donuts. Carnations land at her feet and she smiles at the hoots and applause from the Chancey's Electric Cabaret audience. Moira, Ron and Lou raise their glasses. Before she falls asleep, Norma replays the events of the day in her mind's eye. She lies in bed, steeped in delicious awe at the places where air pockets are found. Some have to be looked for, while others just appear.

VIII

Alison's Story

A chimney sweep clutches a magpie rescued from the chimney breast in our living room.

'Thought it was a pigeon,' he says. 'Magpies don't normally survive for long.'

He rubs the dazed bird's sooty head and coos, 'You're a lucky fella.' The sweep marches towards the open front door, pauses at the porch and says, 'Off you go, mate.'

The freed bird flies towards a powdery grey sky where the clouds hang low and heavy.

'Hope you're prepared for some surprises.' The sweep grins. 'Magpies mean changes in luck, good or bad.'

I smile, but I hate superstition and surprises. The sweep crosses Mount Pleasant Road and gives me a quick nod before climbing into his white van. I wave back and close the front door.

Warren, my husband, walks towards me flashing a copy of *National Geographic* magazine.

'Alison,' he announces, 'you need to hear this.' Bending the spine until the magazine falls open at the centre, he points to the heading at the top of a page. Adjusting his glasses, he reads the opening paragraph.

Records show that Kenneth Johnson's ancestors have lived on Ferris Farm in Cumbria for over 200 years. According to Mr Johnson, his family were unaware of the history of the farm and are delighted to learn of its historical significance. The land on which Ferris Farm is set has witnessed numerous battles throughout England's history, dating back to the Roman invasion.

Given this context, it is perhaps little wonder that Roman relics have been found on Ferris Farm, and these suggest the land was also a place of encampment for Roman soldiers. Mr Johnson could not be persuaded to disclose the amount he and his family have been offered for the bounty of discovered Roman artefacts.

Mr Johnson's discoveries were made possible by a metal detector his eldest son Timothy had bought him as a birthday present.

Warren's thick-lens glasses drift towards the end of his nose.

Staring at me, he asks, 'Well, what do you think?'

Perspiration glistens on the dark-brown skin of his forehead.

'I don't know, what?'

'I would have thought it was pretty obvious. Metal detection, of course. Tottenham has substantial history – God knows what we could find in our garden.'

The garden is ninety by sixty feet and mainly laid to lawn with flower beds on either side. A tall apple tree stands near the patio, providing welcome shade on hot summer days. The russets are rough to the touch but sweet and juicy. I give away lots of apples to my neighbours and like to imagine the fruit satisfying stomachs in the form of pies, crumbles, chutney and jams.

Recently we made an unsuccessful attempt at growing strawberries in the plot behind the shed, and now there is a layer of inedible, pebble-like fruit. Covering the area with round bone-white stones did little to improve appearances as sprouting weeds and the spiky brambles of a dying gooseberry bush now straggle the small area of land.

The garden is one reason why we bought the house. It is west-facing and holds plenty of sunshine all afternoon until the sun sets.

'There could be anything out there, and I'm not just talking about Roman coins,' Warren says, his eyes swivelling. Something has altered in his gaze, as if he has caught sight of something only he can see.

'I've checked on Amazon' – he talks quickly, firing ideas – 'and there's different types of metal detectors we can buy, from the very expensive to those that are frankly tacky and not worth bothering about.'

Since Warren retired, he has joined the Broadwater Farm Choir and spends weekends fishing with other men, but he always comes back grumbling about how the men trick and cheat him. In particular he moans about Charlie Chalk. He says Chalky cheats during the quiz nights and googles the answers each time he visits the toilet.

'Chalky thinks he's better than the rest of us, just because he's got his wedding limousine business and lives in Broxbourne, but who wants to live in Broxbourne? Who in their right mind wants to live in Broxbourne?'

His face dances with excitement. I catch a glimpse of the younger Warren and how he might have been as a teenager, full of scorching, quaking love or raging motorbike frenzy.

'I don't know anything about metal detection, Warren.'

'Well, it's never too late to learn. The starting price is about twenty quid – you can get those ones from Argos – and at the other end you've got detectors that sell for just over a thousand pounds. Those are the super professional types, of course, with highly sophisticated electronic metal detector systems.'

Technical jargon tumbles out of Warren's mouth as he describes the details of each machine, sculpting shapes in the air to demonstrate display screens, nozzles and probes.

'We've got to think about quality and value for money,' he says. 'And there's headphones to consider. Headphones cut down on background noise and make sure you hear the tones of your treasure more easily.'

He makes the word treasure sound definite, chomping down on it, determined to unearth a bounty.

'Well, perhaps we should buy something that's not too expensive and not too... tacky. Is there a middling range?'

'Why bother with the middling range? In for a penny, in for a pound. We have to be serious about this, Alison, otherwise there's no point.'

He takes my hands in his and, lowering his voice, says, 'It's what you call taking a leap of faith.'

We haven't received generous pensions and need to be careful with money; we can't afford to be extravagant. Of course, we have a wish list and an understanding that we will work through each wish, one by one.

At the top of my original wish list was a Caribbean cruise.

We've visited Saint Lucia because that's where our families are from but we've never been to any other Caribbean islands. After we looked carefully at our pension pot, we realised Caribbean cruises were out of reach so I lowered my sights and thought short haul, Europe. I'd settled on a trip to the Borgo Santo Pietro region in Tuscany, where the sweetest bread in the world is made and the recipe's secret is kept in knowing village hands. Cupcake, one of my close friends, has promised to come with me but she's dubious about the merits of Italian bread and says nothing on God's good earth could taste better than her bulla bread.

The metal detector would be the most expensive single purchase we've made since retiring. I look into Warren's watery eyes. He tips his head to one side and gives a begging-bowl smile.

'Please,' he says.

Up until this point our semi-detached household has been snug; like small cogs, we have chugged along to a steady rhythm.

He squeezes my hand and there is a sweaty warmth I want to pull away from.

'You know that I love you, don't you, Alison?' And I smile rather than saying yes, because I don't know. I married Warren believing he loved me but I'm not sure he does anymore. Every now and then I catch him looking at me from the corners of his eyes, sideways looks, grudgingly given and filled with resignation, as if he has backed the wrong horse but will lumber on anyway.

We're not at home when the metal detector arrives. Warren collects the brown cardboard box from Mr and Mrs Norris next door. Carrying it into the living room, he lowers the box and takes a deep breath. He stands with his arms akimbo as if preparing to launch a rocket ship, but I witness a man clutching at a rope. There are many parts to assemble and, talking aloud, Warren coaches himself through the written instructions.

In the kitchen I knead plump, white dough with extra force, pummelling and rolling the mixture until my breathing grows heavy. I pound the flour, olive oil, sea salt and water with all the care and weight I can summon, but I know the bread will taste bad from all the angst that has gone into it.

Once the dough is in the oven, I look down at my hands and see they are trembling. Quickly I wipe them on a tea towel but still they shake, and I glance over at the globe-shaped bottle of Three Barrels brandy standing on the kitchen counter, hidden behind squash and lemonade.

'Alison, Alison, it's ready.'

With a sinking feeling, I walk into the living room where Warren sits on the centre of the rug surrounded by open boxes, sheets of paper and clouds of stiff polythene.

A smile stretches across his face. 'Model 34061. The Cardinal Deluxe. Full Band Spectrum Technology. It's got a three-year warranty. The best on the market! And fully assembled!'

Patches of sweat darken the underarms of his checked shirt and the room smells of his work. I feel dizzy, as if I'm gazing down from the top of a skyscraper not knowing if I will fall. The air is thin and I struggle to breathe.

'Well,' he asks, tenderly stroking the long metal nozzle, 'what do you think?'

It is machinery. Metal bits put together. Expensive machinery on which my husband is pinning his dreams. Something dark flutters inside me, and I remember the sweep and his magpie warning.

'Impressive, very impressive.' I nod, circling Warren and the metal detector as if examining a museum artefact.

'I'll get started,' he says, rolling up his sleeves. 'No time like the present.' Carrying the metal detector, he glides out of the room; gone is his slow-footed trundle. Moving like a much younger man, he clasps the tool horizontally, like a body.

'We should give it a name,' he says.

'It's just a machine,' I say, following him into the kitchen. He stops, his eyes round and bulging, as if I've struck him across the face.

'No, it isn't just a machine, Alison. If that's what you think then you haven't got it at all.' Studying my face, he narrows his eyes. 'No, I can see you don't get it.' He holds up the metal detector and thrusts it towards me. 'This, this, Alison, is a life changer. A dream maker. Your problem is you have no faith and no imagination.'

'I'm trying, Warren. I really am.'

'Are you?'

He sighs and makes his way into the garden. Standing in the centre of the lawn, his proud head held up, fit for a coronation, he says, 'Nefertiti. I'll call her Nefertiti, after the warrior queen.'

Before Warren pulls on his headphones, he calls out, 'You can watch if you want.'

He hovers the machine across our lawn. Pumping and scavenging. There is a terrible craving in the hunch of his body as he swings the detector, dipping and diving, sweeping it low and slow across blades of grass.

'I'm sorry but I've got to nip out,' I shout above the machine's bleeping noise. 'We're running low on groceries. See you later.'

Before I turn away, I note the way Warren's eyes focus on the ground as if he doesn't believe in the soil on which he stands and is determined to plunder and penetrate the earth for everything it is worth.

The groceries are a tub of cholesterol-lowering, low-fat, non-butter spread, a thin-sliced wholemeal loaf and two cartons of semi-skimmed, long-life milk. As I item-hunt along the aisles, my mind drifts and I feel like I am standing in the shadow of the apple tree, observing Warren and his metal detector. What if he finds treasure? Like a solid gold Roman shield, or an amulet garnished with emeralds? I imagine Warren and Nefertiti photographed and featured in newspaper articles, appearing on *The One Show* and earning a mention in *National Geographic*, but I see myself diminish. He has found a new life without me. Ours has been a meek and quiet marriage, a sheltering place in which Warren used to confide in me, telling me about his childhood.

'Mum was a cleaning lady,' he said. 'She cleaned the big houses near Manor House. You know, the ones facing Clissold Park. Dad bought Mum an eternity ring for their fifteenth anniversary. It was beautiful, gold and rubies, but one day Mum came home and said it was gone, that she'd lost it. That evening Mum signed her name on a slip of paper from school agreeing for me to go on a trip to Austria with my classmates… Mum and Dad sacrificed so much so that I'd feel okay. They wanted my whole life to be just one big joyride, as if that would make up for all the things they'd missed, suffered or had to go without.'

When I return from the supermarket Warren is seated at the dining table, typing on his laptop, energy buzzing around him like static electricity.

'I think there's something near the apple tree,' he says, without looking up. 'I've dug as much as I could and found this.' He holds up a broken key ring. Without commenting I dart into the kitchen and switch on the patio lights. A huge mound of earth is piled to the side of the tree and a deep hole dug around its base, exposing its roots.

Walking back into the living room, I speak to Warren as if he is a child with a fever.

'No, not the apple tree, Warren. We mustn't disturb the apple tree.'

'Don't be a spoilsport, Alison. You'll kick yourself if that tree is sitting on a treasure trove.'

'I can see you've explored quite a lot of ground already. If there was anything underneath the tree you would have found it by now.'

'Now that's where you're wrong. This is a craft and like all crafts it takes patience and concentration. You can't hurry these things. Slow and easy does it.'

There is nothing easy about any of this. As I set the table for dinner, knives and forks are slapped down, drawers are rammed shut and the loaf of bread is burnt to charcoal, sinking like a brick to the bottom of the litter bin. Warren is no different to miners struck by the Gold Rush; most of them rotted by the roadside.

Soon the lawn is pockmarked, a potential playground for hedgehogs and moles. Squirming on their backs with no hope of turning over, insects are scorched by the sun. Warren has filled a steel pail with his findings. Iron nails, a spanner, a shovel part, a belt buckle and a small, empty paint can. Gollum-like, he clings onto his precious, muttering about the magnificence of gravity while his boots blacken the ivory-white kitchen floor tiles.

Over breakfast Warren says very little and pushes away his plate of buttered toast.

'You okay?' I ask.

He frowns. 'I know there's important stuff out there. There has to be.'

When I hear the shower I guess that Warren is going out. Before he closes the front door, he calls out, 'Bye.' He doesn't say where he is going as he usually does – but then nothing is 'usual' anymore.

In the late afternoon Warren breezes into the living room, offering me a bunch of violet-coloured chrysanthemums. I've told him many times I don't like the funereal associations of this flower, but he must have forgotten.

Performing a little hop and skip, he pulls me to my feet.

'Yellow suits you,' he says.

Locking his arms round my waist, he presses his lips against mine and dips his tongue inside my mouth. It is a long time since we've kissed and touched; I've forgotten what to do and let my arms fall limply by my side. As if he has remembered something, Warren stops and steps back, wiping his mouth with the back of his hand. His eyes race about the floor as he brushes his fingers through the tight, dark curls of his hair.

'Dinner smells good,' he says.

'Moussaka. Thought I'd try something different.'

The next Sunday is sunny, but there is a nip in the air. Tall towers of ironed clothes deck the living room sofa and the air smells of White Flowers spray starch. I keep my head down, falling in with the pressure and weight of the iron, forcing it along seams and driving it hard against creases.

'Close your eyes,' Warren whispers, his head poking round the living-room door. He takes slow steps towards me, his hands held behind his back.

His clothes are covered in grass and earth stains and I fret about the dirt he is treading into the carpet. I don't want to close my eyes; I don't want to go any further into the darkness.

'Go on, close your eyes,' he coaxes and I do.

He chortles. 'Okay, you can open them now.'

I stare into the nest he has made by lacing his hands together. In Warren's palms is a small gold pocket watch. Clumps of earth cling to its case but beneath the mud is a burnished, honeyed splendour. 'It's beautiful,' I say. 'This is incredible, Warren.'

'I'll clean it off. Must be worth a bob or two... Told you I'd find something. Can't wait to see Chalky's face when he hears about this.' He leaves the room whistling. 'We've got Nefertiti to thank for this. I knew it, I knew we were on to a winner.'

Weeks gallop by and Warren and Nefertiti appear in the *Enfield and Haringey Independent* and the *Tottenham Community Press* under the headlines 'Tottenham's Buried Treasure' and 'Senior Citizen's Lucky Strike'. I have a small mention: 'and wife'.

'I'm turning into a bit of a celebrity,' Warren titters after a photo shoot with the *Tottenham and Wood Green Independent*. He complains that the shirt I've ironed is too stiff.

'I think this shirt is wearing me, not the other way round,' he jokes.

Cockerel-like he struts, sucking in his stomach and posturing in front of the mirror.

'What do you think? Silver fox or sad old black man?' He laughs a new laugh.

'Ally, do I look okay?' he asks. He hasn't called me Ally in years.

'Yes, you look fine but your shoelaces are undone... again.'

Tutting, he bends down to tie loose, hurried knots. Before he retired, Warren's laces were always done and his leather shoes mirror-shiny.

'I've been asked to give a talk at the girls' school,' he says.
'When?'

'September. It'll give me time to prepare overheads, photographs. The teacher who phoned said they're hoping to set up a local metal detectorists club.'

'That's good.'

'Little acorns, Alison. Little acorns.'

He leaps upstairs, taking two steps at a time. Gone is his arthritis. He's going to a seminar at the local historical society where he will show off his find. The watch is kept in a cream-coloured, satin-lined box in a cabinet drawer. For a time I wished Warren had found a ruby-studded gold eternity band, but the watch is ours, a fresh delight. Not a helmet, not a sword but a watch. For so small an object it ticks very loudly. I run my fingers along its intricate engravings. There is flecked, looped edging and a detailed image of a galleon ship in the centre of the case.

It is an Elgin watch, dated 1873 and valued at five thousand pounds. It has a pearly white face, fifteen jewels, black Arabic numbers and a tiny winding stem at the twelve o'clock position. Not gold-plated but eighteen-carat gold. Warren says that the valuation report suggests the watch has a maritime history and was once important in navigation. I wonder about its first owner, perhaps a ship's captain, and the many seas the watch has sailed. I have caught gold fever, singing and supping Warren's every kiss. On Sunday morning I will make my first attempt at metal detection under his careful supervision.

'Ally,' Warren calls from upstairs, 'can you get Jonty Winthrop's card from my wallet? I can't remember his address and I've promised to pick him up.'

Warren's brown calf-leather wallet is fat with business

cards from his newly acquired contacts. In the wallet's centre fold is a crumpled slip of paper – a receipt. I flatten it and read:

'Men's pocket watch. Circa 1873. Eighteen carat. £4,500. Purchased 29 June 2019. Simpsons Antiques, Jewellers and Pawnbrokers. Ipswich.'

I have never been bundled into the back of a truck but I feel as if I have been now. My body shakes and sand coats the insides of my mouth and throat. Quickly I return the receipt to the fold and take out the card with Jonty Winthrop's address, placing it on the small table in the hallway.

'Jonty's card is on the table,' I call out.

'Thanks, love,' he shouts down. I hear him whistling.

Sitting in an armchair, I pick at the rough ends of the worn armrests. Warren has lied and cheated. He's dented our retirement money by buying the most expensive metal detector he could find and a watch he pretends he has found in our garden. I remember his dancing feet and how I caught gold fever, forgiving the potholes and torn lawn.

Our silver-framed wedding photograph sits on the mantelpiece. It was taken forty years ago outside St Benet Fink Church on Walpole Road. I wonder what became of the children we never had. Large, gaping holes in our garden resemble waiting burial plots, and our unborn children are the buried treasure; along with all our hopes and dreams, they lie asleep in the soil.

Warren whistles while I pluck at the loose skin on my elbow and tears roll down my face. It is then that I hear him fall, tumbling down the staircase, his body thudding against steps and banisters – and then there is silence, stillness. I can't move my arms or legs. Shocks pile up like boulders, one on top of the other. He calls my name.

Each time I try to raise a limb I picture Warren reaching for a pile of notes pushed under a cashier's screen in the Co-operative bank. Notes tucked into a brown envelope and slipped inside a jacket pocket. All the things beneath, all the things buried between us.

He calls my name again.

My body moves, but not towards the hallway. I creep through the French doors into the garden and throw up by the apple tree. The evening air cools my face and neck. Heading to the side of the house, I tread the narrow, stony path separating our house from the next. Warren will call my name until he runs out of voice or until he dies; my name will be the last word he speaks and I will be the last person or thing he wants.

It is late evening when I get back and find Warren where he has fallen. He lies helplessly on his back, like the insects he tossed aside in our garden. Dried blood marks his forehead. He breathes faintly and turns his head to face me when I bend down.

'I was calling,' he whispers. 'Where were you?'

I don't answer but tell him to rest his voice while I call for help. Every small movement makes him wince. When the paramedics arrive in suits of forest green, I am reassured I won't have to deal with Warren alone. He tries to hold my fingers as he lies on the stretcher, but I prise them away. In the ambulance he mumbles and I lower my head to listen.

'Nef...' he murmurs, his voice hoarse.

'Sorry, darling, I can't make out what you're saying.'

'Nefert...'

'Nef? Do you mean never, Warren? I can't understand you, darling.'

'Nefertiti...' he repeats softly but clearly. 'Nefertiti.'

'Nef? ...Never? Never it? I'm sorry but I can't understand, Warren. Shh, try not to talk – rest. Just rest your voice.' I pat his hands and smile at the paramedic.

Warren had tripped over his shoelaces; he's fractured his pelvis and is advised to rest following surgery. After two weeks they send him home. How withered he looks. His foolish schemes have swallowed him whole. The loose brown skin on his face sags and droops around his jaws and neck, and I almost miss the younger, slippery, arthritis-free trickster. The young man with the sprightly steps has disappeared and been replaced with this husk.

On Saturday I leave Warren with Angela from number five, and when I return he is sleeping; he is shrunken and his head rests on the pillow.

'How has he been?' I ask, pulling off my coat. The bedroom smells of puke and medicine.

'Fine. He's had some chicken broth and a roll. Looks like he's getting his appetite back. He's still groggy, though – must be the painkillers.'

'Yes, must be the painkillers.'

'Try not to worry, Alison. He'll be up and about in no time, you'll see. I best be getting back,' she says and stands to put on her bulky pink parka.

'Thanks, Angela. You've been a godsend, don't know what I would do without you.'

'No probs, I'm happy to help.'

Angela makes her way downstairs and quietly closes the front door behind her.

Sitting beside the bed, I watch Warren's eyes flicker beneath their lids. His mouth falls open, revealing a deep red hollow. I look away and stare down at my hands. Twisting my plump fingers, I realise the only useful thing I can make with them is bread. Bread. Bread you can buy from any shop. I wonder if I have any purpose at all. Pulling the brandy bottle from my cardigan pocket, I swallow deep mouthfuls until the heat stretches beyond my throat, warming my body and softening the room's corners and edges.

'Ally,' Warren says my name like newly discovered land.

'Yes, Warren, I'm here.' His name is heavy in my mouth.

'Where have you been?'

'Ipswich.' My eyes never leave his.

He swallows hard. 'Ipswich?'

'Yes, Ipswich, Warren.' I watch him squirm, and again I'm reminded of the dying insects in our back garden, baked by the sun.

He coughs, his voice dry. 'You know, Ally, I think Dad forgave Mum about that ring. I think he understood...'

I stand up and with the flats of my hands I brush the knife pleats in my skirt.

'Forgiveness is important, isn't it, Ally?'

'I'll make you a cup of tea,' I say and tuck the thin bedsheet tightly into the sides of the mattress before plumping up the duvet. 'You must be thirsty.'

He tries to sit up but the pain makes him flinch. 'I'm asking you to forgive me. Surely I deserve your forgiveness, Ally. I am a good man. I am a good man.'

I leave the bedroom and head downstairs. I've returned the watch and paid the money into our account. I will have my Borgo Santo Pietro holiday and eat rosemary and olive bread, warmed by a kind, Tuscan sun. Warren and I are passengers in a boat, and somehow I will keep us afloat. I've recovered and restored what he took. Our lawn is now covered in new Cumberland turf that coats the soil like a lush blue-green ocean, and my apple tree stands tall and strong.

I've tried to call my young friend Binty, but there's no reply. I need to tell her about my unbuckling and this foolish panning for gold. She's surprisingly wise for her years and I know she'll understand. No-nonsense Cupcake will only think of me as a fool. I laugh to myself because there is no one else to hear – to think I might have gone up in the world, got lucky, had my happy ever after. Binty is right, animals and people are not so different; hunger and instinct drive us all.

The metal detector was stored in a cupboard with the vacuum cleaner but is now trussed in bubble wrap. Forcing it into a cardboard box, I seal all the sides of the parcel with sturdy black duct tape. The manufacturers were very understanding and will return most but not all of the money; they have to take into consideration the fact that the merchandise has been used. The Customer Service Officer I spoke with about our faulty metal detector said, 'Well, in that case, a small refund is the least we can do. After all, we like to keep our customers happy.' At the post office, the counter clerk wears a badge that says his name is Clive.

'Good morning, how can I help?' Clive says. He probably sees just another weary old black woman, a little overweight. I want to tell him I once had ambitions and dreams.

Lifting the box, I say, 'I need to send this by special delivery.'

'Right, pop it on the scales. Still raining, is it? It was pouring this morning when I came to work.'

'I didn't notice.' Brandy coats my breath and slurs my words. I'm aware that I'm a little unsteady; the man's features become fuzzy.

Clive raises his eyes. 'You didn't notice the rain?'

My woollen coat is wet and damp hair covers my head. The post office walls spin slowly around me.

He stares at me, a deep frown making a groove in his forehead.

'Special delivery, is it?' he says stiffly, judgement hardening his eyes.

'Yes,' I mumble, 'special delivery.' I can't say 'delivery' properly – the 'v' turns into a 'w' no matter how hard I try. Clive shakes his head, mutters something under his breath.

Opening my purse, I fiddle for loose change. My mouth is dry, my hands are shaking and no, I didn't notice the weather at all.

IX

Cupcake's Story

I'm on my way to my mum's house, carrying Sainsbury's carrier bags bulging with groceries. Root vegetables, spices, herbs, rice; enough to make her a dinner that will last a few days. My arms feel like logs of timber, but I continue walking alongside Downhills Park towards her house, my eyes following the clay-coloured henna leaf prints that tattoo the autumn pavements.

'Hi Cupcake,' Binty Larson says as she walks by. She's on her way to visit her parents who live in Lympne block on the Farm. A bristling wind's blowing and she's shivering because she's not dressed warmly enough. Jeans and a meagre hoodie won't keep out the cold. Young people, I don't know.

'Haven't seen you for a while. How are you, Binty?'

'I'm fine,' she says but her big hazel eyes well with water; I can see she's been crying. I've known Binty since she was a bump in her mum's belly.

Pulling her hood more closely around her head, she says she's sorry but she can't stop and talk, she's in a hurry. I tell her it's nice to see her and to take good care. Binty and Ruth were happy, well-behaved kids. Now they're young women making their way in the world and I know they, too, will have to manage the curveballs life throws at them.

Mum opens the front door to the hallway just enough so that I have to step in sideways like a crab. Turning away, she shuffles back to the living room in flattened-down slippers. Everything is done very slowly because I need to be patient with us both. She has carers who visit her daily but I also spend time with her.

'Cupcake, you're late,' she calls out.

In the hallway I remove my coat and retrieve one sleepy sock that has got stuck in the bottom of a boot. I hang my heavy coat over the banister, though I know she'll hate seeing it there, a heavy darkness spoiling clean lines. The shopping bags slump beside a tall cupboard in the kitchen, and I tie back my hair to avoid netting any cooking smells. When I walk into the living room I find Mum wrapped up tightly in her old wine-coloured brushed-cotton dressing gown. Lodged in the sofa, she's become part of the upholstery; she clutches a red rubber hot water bottle that's missing its fleecy cover.

'My back's killing me,' she says.

'Have you put your heat pad on?'

'Yes, but it doesn't make any difference. The doctor says it's wear and tear. What can you do about wear and tear?'

Returning to the kitchen, I chop the vegetables and pop the stew on the stove.

'Ready for your bath?' I ask.

Holding her arms, I help her up from the sofa and very slowly we climb the staircase.

'Who would have thought I'd come to this?' she asks.

In her bedroom she sits on the side of the bed that faces

the windows. Her skin is silken, the colour of candle wax. Her body shape is the same as mine, and I see what I will become.

'You know, I wasn't always like this,' she says, and I hear the younger woman laughing, see her dancing and being swept off her feet by my dad.

'I had my moments,' she sniffs.

The blue bath seat lowers her into the tub and I struggle with the shower head. She shivers at the cold; she prefers the water to be fire-hot. As Mum lathers her body with her favourite Damask Rose soap, she remarks on its lovely smell and says that it doesn't dry her skin like the others do.

'All done,' I say.

'You're a good girl,' she says like a kind-natured drunk. I help her out of the bath and we return to the bedroom. The peach-coloured bath towel I've taken from the airing cupboard is fluffy and warm, and I rub it over her body.

'Feeling better?' I ask.

She nods and, staring at me, says, 'You look like your Aunt Eva.'

I feel her examining my face.

'It's all right,' she says, 'I'm just remembering.'

She lets me 'L'Oréal' her face and dry her hair.

'Don't know why you bother,' she says. 'I look like an old witch and there's no fixing that.'

Pulling the elasticised socks over her swollen ankles takes time.

'I don't think your dad ever said he loved me,' she says. 'Now why do you suppose that was?'

'I don't know, Mum.'

'And don't give me all that about him not being good with words. He was good enough with words when he wanted to be.'

Carefully, we walk back downstairs. When she settles into a nest of cushions in her armchair, I serve her a bowl of vegetable stew with a buttered roll and a mug of sweetened hot cocoa.

She says the stew I've cooked is good. 'You never learned this from me.' She almost smiles.

'You were a very good cook,' I say, and she stops eating and searches my face.

'Was I? Really?'

'Yes, you were... are.'

'It's all right,' she says and shakes her head, 'I'm just remembering. I do a lot of that now.'

'You will remember not to put the stew in the fridge until it's properly cooled down, won't you?' I ask.

'What?' she says. She never hears my questions, only my answers to her questions. In the living room I sit down beside her.

'I'm going now, Mum.'

Leaning over, I kiss her forehead and stroke her fine silver hair.

'But you didn't answer my question,' she says. 'Why do you think your dad never told me that he loved me?'

'Love's a verb, Mum. Perhaps he showed it. Just because he didn't say it doesn't mean he didn't feel it.'

'All those years,' she says. 'But men didn't say it back then. It's just that it matters now. I'm trying to sort out the pieces left over.' She lowers her head. 'It's the last blanket I need.

'It's all right,' she continues. 'You're not to worry about me. I've got too much time to think. Go before it rains.'

The sky is crystal-clear, blue and cloudless, but she tells me to take an umbrella.

'There's a few brollies under the stairs. You never know...

Have you got time for a story?' she asks. Glancing at the clock I realise I've stayed longer than I wanted to, but I like listening to Mum's stories.

'It all came back to me the other night,' she says. 'I had this craving. Worst ever. Thing is I could taste the stuff in my mouth, on my tongue. Strangest thing. Bread pudding. It started off with bread pudding,' she says, smiling. 'I couldn't remember who taught me how to make it.'

Mum always used to make bread puddings.

'Took me the longest time to remember. It was your godmother, Betty, who taught me. I can still see her with her bright red hair, popping raisins into her mouth. Where do you think she got all that hair? And what was the point of all that glory when most of the time she hid it under a scarf?'

'She was glamorous, though – and what a singing voice. She was brilliant in *Annie Get Your Gun*,' I say.

My godmother belonged to an amateur operatic society and I'd seen her perform, her voice belting around the auditorium. Mum looks at me.

'Things were different when you were born. Very different. You know, I've never quite worked out why they call the past "the old days". They can't be the old days, can they? The world was younger then. So they've got that wrong. Those were the young days and these are the old days.'

She pulls up her woollen blanket and covers her knees.

'I loved your dad something silly. I'd always liked a certain sort of man. The cheeky, handsome ones that came at you with their low whistling. I don't know why, because my dad, your grandad, was so strait-laced, cautious, upright, but your dad walked into my life and that was it. All change.'

My parents arrived in the UK in 1954 having sailed from Kingston, Jamaica on an Italian liner called the Fair Seas. When they disembarked at Plymouth it was raining heavily. They were not wearing coats and carried two small leather suitcases. Greeted by the squeaks and blasts of a loud brass band playing *Rule Britannia*, they settled in Mother England.

'The night you were born was a dreadful night – the weather. It snowed and snowed, I'd never known such cold.'

I know the day that I was born was a very bleak day in British sporting history. 6 February 1958. It was the night the Busby Babes lost their lives in a plane crash, and I was busy being born. Matt Busby's young footballers plunged to their tragic, untimely deaths and the news was spread across the front page of every national newspaper the following day. Their bodies were still strapped to their passenger seats, pitted in the snow.

'1958 was also the year of Laurel Aitken and "Boogie in My Bones". Your dad could really dance, he was good enough for *Strictly Come Dancing*. You should have seen him, Cupcake.'

And in my mind's eye I can see my parents gliding across the living room. Their kitten-heel and wingtip shoes using every inch of mauve linoleum floor. Their lithe fluid-limbed bodies rocking, reeling, whooping and bouncing on the high notes. A bluesy saxophone blowing woozy smoke rings until the early hours of Sunday morning.

Her voice grows small. 'No one talked to us back then. A black man and a white woman married and setting up home. There was a lot of hatred. No blacks, no Irish, no dogs. Vile Teddy boys. Nasty things put through our letter box. Dog turds, sanitary pads.'

The daily indignities chipped away but they kept going.

'Your Dad was told to go back home, small change was dropped in his hand each time he shopped like he had leprosy and he was turned down for job after job, having to take any odd scrap of work he could find so we could survive. They were hard, bitter days.'

At the time, my godmother lived with her husband and family at the other end of Harringay Road where Mum and Dad lived. Betty befriended my mum one morning when Mum was sweeping the garden path. She was the only neighbour on the road to talk to my mother.

Mum continues, her voice full of new notes, 'My waters broke. I remember I was standing in the bathroom brushing my teeth and I knew you were on your way. In the morning I'd carried a sack of potatoes from the vegetable rack and I'd put terrible strain on my stomach. God knows what I was thinking, but that's the thing, you don't always think, do you? I called out and your dad came running. I was on all fours in terrible pain. He didn't know what to do, he was panicking, and then he ran out of the house and said he would try to call an ambulance. Only one man on the road had a phone. This was 1958, remember. Your dad knocked on Mr Bateman's front door and asked to use the phone, Mr Bateman said something about not helping a nigger and shut the door in his face. Then he ran down to Betty's house. He didn't know her name, we didn't really know them, but your dad was desperate. They were there before your dad could wink. Betty's husband, Sid, sat with your dad while she helped me give birth.

'You were a difficult birth and when you did show your face, Betty was the first person you saw. You were as quiet as a mouse and only cried when she slapped your bum. Betty and I began a lifelong friendship and she became your godmother. It was dear Betty who taught me how to make bread pudding.'

Mum had been a fighter, boxing at life. Headstrong and spirited, but quiet and distilled beside me now in her smaller, seasoned form. I've got photographs of her in miniskirts and tight trousers, and ones of my dad wearing bell-bottoms and an afro like a halo.

'I know it wasn't easy for you. I remember when you'd just started secondary school and I came home and caught you.' Her face darkens.

Stavroulla Papamichael had told me that the back of my neck was black and dirty, so when I got home from school I threw off my blazer and ran into the bathroom, where I scoured my neck with Ajax until my skin bled and my fingers trembled. I tried to scrub the names from my memory: rubber-lips, nig-nog, blackie, jungle-bunny, sambo, wog, shit-face. Mum found me there. She cried as she gently sponged and dried my broken, bloody skin.

My parents met in St James, Jamaica in 1946. Dad had returned from the US following the Second World War and Mum was teaching in a secondary school. Dad was a chiselled black man and Mum was the white great-great-granddaughter of slave owners. It was love, taboo and excitement at first sight. Mum's father forbade the relationship but Mum said, 'If he's no son of yours, then I'm no daughter.' My parents married despite all Mum's family's threats and protestations. And then there I was – their beloved daughter Cupcake.

They settled in north London, saved hard until they bought their own house in Tottenham. Dad worked twelve-hour shifts in a glass bottle factory until a machine accident nearly cost him an eye.

He died seven years ago. Dementia, the thief with a big black bag, stole him away. Before his diagnosis, there was a pre-dementia time when the condition seeded, taking slow root, snipping at his heels and feeding him fanciful ideas about what was possible. He wanted to buy an ice-cream van but all Mum could see were reasons not to.

'What do ice-cream men actually do in winter, besides starve?' she said.

'That's it, snuff out my good idea,' Dad said.

Then Dad did the unforgiveable thing. He died. Mum called him selfish, stupid, careless. She gave all his clothes away to the Cancer Research charity shop on Friday and banged on the shop door the following Monday, wanting them all back.

Mum stirs and wakes. She wipes the dribble from her mouth.

'You still here?'

'Yes, but I'm leaving now.'

'I look at you sometimes,' she says in an unsure voice. 'You're the job I've done. Did I do okay?'

With my biggest smile, I answer, 'Yeah, you did good.'

'H'mm.' She looks me up and down, then, sighing, looks out the window and starts moaning about pigeons and the mess they make.

I kiss her on the forehead and put on my coat and boots in the hall.

'See you on Friday,' I call out as I open the front door.

'And say hello to that young Ricky for me, tell him to keep reaching for those stars,' she says.

'I will, Mum. I will.'

X

Binty's Story

Binty's family are the kind of people who mow down a mountain if it stands in their way. They are quietly determined types who, on spotting a means to an end, seize it. Although Binty left her family and Broadwater Farm behind years ago, she likes to believe she carries her family's spirit of resolve with her.

A car with strong headlights drifts along Cinderwick Road, dusting light on the drooping lips of the stone steps that lead up to the front door of number fourteen. The time on Binty's watch reads 9.45pm and if she stays any longer she'll oversleep and be late for work tomorrow. Her feet are cold, her hands are cold, and twice she's been asked by late-night cruisers if she's doing 'business', but her eyes never shift from the silhouetted figures that move behind the thin curtains of Flat 4, 14 Cinderwick Road, Crouch End. The figures come together and pull apart. Binty will wait until the lights are turned off – the ceiling light and the side lamp. The Tiffany Dragonfly side lamp with missing garnet eyes. Dan bought it from an antique shop in Camden Passage a year ago.

'Will you look at that?' he said, balancing the heavy lamp on the side table and then standing back, his face creased with the effort of lifting.

'Well?' he asked, staring at Binty.

She shrugged and carried on munching salt and vinegar crisps. 'Don't do ornaments, Dan.'

'This is serious baroque, Binty,' Dan said as Binty walked into the kitchen to put on the kettle.

'Coffee?' she called out, only to hear the front door close.

The walls of Flat 4, 14 Cinderwick Road, Crouch End are covered in framed photographs chronicling Dan's travels. Dancing with the dead in Madagascar. Perched beside the Moai on Easter Island. Stooping in a Borneo garden as he points to a rare, stinking flower, Rafflesia Arnoldii. The plant's circular head and surrounding petals are the size of a Dunlop tyre. Rafflesia arnoldii only blooms every seven years and smells like death. In the photograph a self-satisfied smirk dapples Dan's face. When Binty asked him why he dashed around the world searching for the rare and the wild, Dan stopped and looked at the space above her head that he increasingly talked to. 'Same reason why boys climb trees: adventure.' He stopped travelling after his last stint in Mozambique when he fractured his right fibula abseiling. Binty concluded he had run out of world.

Binty liked Dan's mother Olivia. She had an owl-like wisdom about her. Dan's parents divorced years ago; his dad, Brian, didn't have much to say for himself. Dan referred to him as 'the old boy'. Brian and his new wife Anne lived in Holland-on-Sea, and when Binty spent the Easter holidays with them two years ago, Brian pinched her bottom and pleaded early-onset dementia. Dan sniggered, saying, 'It's all right, Pops, no harm done. No harm done, eh, Binty?' And she didn't know what to say or think. Anne retreated into the kitchen where she broke at least three china plates and apologised for her 'butterfingers'.

The shadowed figures come together, their limbs and separateness disappearing. Binty looks away and down the length of the dark and familiar Crouch End Street. Standing on the opposite side of the road, grateful for nights like this when the sky is empty of an exposing moon. Once a week she finds herself looking up at the windows of the same flat, searching for the beginning or a proper ending to the ball of matted emotional string that was her relationship with Dan.

Only a year earlier, their damp bodies would crumble Pringles into the living room shag pile; afterwards, they would eat hungrily from the same can of cold baked beans. The warmth of his slumbering body beside hers gave Binty comfort and reassurance; she even grew comfortable with the trumpeting earthiness of his farts. Throwing out caution and inhibition, she thought she might keep Dan, trusting they would go the distance. Her parents' relationship was as old as wood and she thought she could have the same.

She knows people who don't understand her will call her behaviour stalking. It is hard to accept that what she does is criminal, but the act of watching or following someone over a period of time is just that, stalking – and illegal. She tells herself she means no harm; she doesn't harass, intimidate or threaten. Dan doesn't even know she's there. One evening a car alarm pierced the night air and he pulled aside a curtain to peer through the living-room window. He seemed unaware of Binty's reduction to a spectral presence skulking on the opposite side of the street.

It's not like she's a hunter or a predator, because all along she was Dan's prey, Dan's victim. Binty thinks a better description would be OLD, obsessive love disorder, which affects about 0.1 per cent of adults. Even after reading mountains of books aimed at helping people move on from unhealthy relationships, she still finds herself walking to 14 Cinderwick Road and looking up at the windows of Flat 4.

Dan's car is parked outside; a black Skoda that needs washing. Binty tries hard to forget the back seat. She remembers the upholstery, the flooring and the small tell-tale spotlight in the roof that used to turn their carnal faces feral.

R&B sounds spill out from a nearby coffee and snack bar wedged between We Luv Nails and The Hair Gallery at the junction at the end of the road. The bar's chairs and tables are occupied by transport workers from nearby Hornsey railway station.

Her attention returns to the flat when she hears the front door shutting. A woman walks down the path, heaves the rusty iron gate behind her and crosses the road. Binty smells the woman's sharp citrus perfume as she passes by, walking jauntily, her heels making a clickety-click sound, as if she possesses a hidden, precious birthright about which Binty knows nothing.

Binty's parents originally came from Hagworthingham, known as Hag, in Lincolnshire, where according to her mother nothing much happened. They were farming people; in their world little separated one day from another. That was why her parents, as soon as they turned sixteen, left Hag for the busyness and spark of London, preferring factory work to farming. They live in Lympne block on the Farm, but Binty now rents a flat in Stroud Green. Her parents didn't say much when she was growing up so she is used to silence, stillness and waiting. They were people of few words and when they spoke, they were precise. Her mother once said, 'In the country, people let their surroundings and the cycle of seasons, cattle, crops, land and light speak for them and shape their lives. It was our way of keeping steady and sane – we didn't trust anything outside of the land and the natural motion of things. I'm not saying that farming is easy – it isn't – but we belonged to the land, it didn't belong to us.' Her family have always had a core that solders them to nature, to its capacity to form them and their capacity to shape it. This has given them a certainty and a toughness that they brought with them to Broadwater Farm. Binty's maternal grandparents still have a small sugar beet holding. They keep chickens, goats and sheep. When they were children, she and her sister Ruth spent summer holidays with their grandparents, but she would count the days until she returned to her home in Tottenham, to the Farm, with its pace, pulse and rhythm.

The woman who just left the flat suddenly trips and the contents of her handbag roll across the pavement. Binty suspects some weakness in the woman's ankles. Coins, polo mints, a packet of paper tissues, an Oyster card, keys, lipstick and a light bulb which rolls into the gutter. A light bulb?

The woman scrambles for her belongings. In the amber light of the lamp post, the woman's mascara train-tracks make her look like a lost clown. Binty approaches the woman, pretending she cares, and asks, 'You okay?' The woman nods, then shakes her head and begins to sob. A long, stretching ladder tears the woman's tights, and Binty gawps at the suddenness of the woman's grazed bare skin.

'No. I'm okay, really,' the woman says, but her tears fall all the same.

'Do you need to sit down?' Binty asks. The woman allows her to take her arm and lead her to the snack bar at the bottom of the road. The fluorescent light in the bar is bright and blinding but Binty is able to see her better. The woman's face is pin-cushion round. Dan always maintained that he preferred cheekbones, not freckles, but this woman's face is spat full of freckles like she's been standing too close to a frying pan. A waiter saunters over. His tired, pinched face says, 'Why don't you bugger off so we can lock up and go home?'

'Two coff—'

'No, tea for me,' the woman interrupts.

'Of course, two teas,' Binty quietly agrees.

The woman draws a white tissue from her handbag, wipes her eyes and blows her nose.

'It's been a rotten night. From start to finish,' the woman says.

As if knocking for answers, the woman raps her fingers on the table. 'What is it with men, anyway?' she says, fixing Binty with solemn eyes.

Binty smiles.

'Ha.' Shaking her head the woman starts wagging her finger. 'I'll tell you one thing...' And then she stops.

Binty feels like she's committing a bank robbery and fiddling with the safe. High-voltage prickles pulse through her body.

'Relationships aren't easy,' she offers and the woman nods. Her black-and-white corporate clothes are restrained and formal but her crisp, lemony perfume boils over and works too hard. What was it Dan used to say about subtlety?

'Rough night, then? Fell out with your boyfriend?' Binty prompts.

The woman sighs, looks out through the window. 'Yeah, had a row with my boyfriend. We're passionate people, you see. He's got a temper on him and so have I.'

'All couples argue. I mean none of us are perfect, are we?' Binty says. The woman doesn't respond and Binty isn't sure if she's heard her or isn't listening.

'I live round here,' Binty continues. 'Ran low on milk. My cat...' but Binty doesn't own a cat; her lies flow like honey. 'She's a stray, a great big thing. A tabby. I found her on my doorstep one morning. Molly.'

'Aw, that's sweet. I like cats,' the woman says. 'I don't have one but I like them.'

Somewhere out back there's a door that keeps banging and a large, unmoving dog sits like a downtrodden rug by the counter, forcing everyone to either step over or around it.

Glancing around, the woman sips at her tea. 'What's this place called?'

'Mugs and Hugs,' Binty answers.

The tea is sweet and strong. 'I needed this,' the woman says. She leaves a faint press of dark plum lipstick on the cup's rim. She's the colour of the strong tea Binty's drinking. Noticing her long, thick hair, Binty wants to lean forward, grab her head and wrench at the glossy black extensions, but instead she sits on her hands and mumbles about the cold.

Dan used to tell Binty not to paint her face, dye her hair or lose weight. A year after moving in to Flat 4, he lost his job writing a weekly local newspaper column, and somehow it was Binty's fault.

'You're always there, in my space, moving my things. I feel like I'm being suffocated.'

Their living together became a capoeira of frenzied make-up sex and muck throwing. Dan grumbled about Binty's old women's knickers and Binty moaned about his nightly pneumatic-drill snoring. They topped and tailed until they were left with a bloodless, wavering midriff. By winter, Dan had decided Binty had lost her point in his life.

'There's just too much of you, Binty. Have you never heard of bite-sized pieces? Your clothes, your shoes, your boxes, your bags. Your things – you've taken over.' And then, looking at the space above her head, he said, 'And to be frank, what's really killed us is your lack of empathy as much as anything else. You just don't get me.'

When she returned home from work one day her suitcases had been packed and left at the top of the staircase.

'I think that's everything,' Dan said as if talking to a removal man.

A week later, Binty phoned her mother. 'I'm very sorry, pet, but you were bound to burn your fingers with that one,' her mother said. 'To be honest, your dad and I never really liked him. You and Ruth and your choices – I just don't understand it. We gave you a stable upbringing, we've always been here for you, so why are you both so blind to your worth? Dan was way too full of himself. You need to stick to your own kind, Binty, the sort of men you can depend on.'

Binty isn't sure what her kind is. Should she decide on the grounds of age, education, social class, ethnicity, neighbourhood, beliefs, values, politics? She used to think love cancelled out everything. Dan left her with muddles and mess, the kind of soggy mess that remains when you're done wringing chickens' necks. For the last ten months she has watched the flat and Dan's movements. She rifles through her replacements. Women. Tall. Short. Plump. Thin. Young. Not-so-young. Older. Black. Asian. White. Mixed heritage. Latina.

The woman slurps her tea. 'He's told me about his exes. The last serious one he had was really difficult. Clingy, he said, you know the type. Said he felt sorry for her – some women just don't know when to walk away.' Using her index finger and thumb, she pulls a strand of hair from between her lips.

'No, I suppose not.'

'She had a weird name, sounded like a washing-up liquid. What was it?' She screws up her eyes as if this will jog her memory.

'There are always two sides to a story though, aren't there?'

The woman circles her finger in the air. 'Uh uh, this one was screwy – I mean seriously damaged. Mental health problems, bit of a bunny boiler by all accounts. Sent him texts begging him to take her back, try again.'

Binty swallows hard. She did no such thing.

'She wanted kids but she wasn't emotionally stable, and Dan said she wasn't a looker either. Too fond of cakes and puddings. Sounds bitchy but he said on her death certificate it'll say 'death by cake'. Ha. Sometimes we women are our own worst enemy. You've got to stay lean if you want to keep them keen.'

Binty bites into the little chocolate biscuit in her saucer but struggles to eat it.

'No, she definitely wasn't the one.' The woman shakes her head.

'And you are?'

Like a cat who's got the cream, the woman grins. 'Yes, yours truly. You have to know how to reel 'em in.'

She leans forward and points to herself.

'Whore in the bedroom, Nigella in the kitchen. Dan can't get enough of my boozy Beef Wellington.'

The woman breathes through her genitals. Binty feels like she's about to vomit tea and biscuit all over the table.

This is the first of Dan's girlfriends Binty has spoken with. She knows there are no answers to be found in red wine, in horoscopes or in listening to this woman's prattle.

'It was one of those whirlwind things with us, you know,' the woman says and does a quick, jazz hands thing, but all Binty grasps is how slowly the weeks and months have passed.

Binty cups her hands around the mug. Studying the woman's manicured nails, she hides her own.

'I couldn't help but notice the light bulb,' she says.

'Oh, that's for his beloved Tiffany lamp. He's had all the red garnet bug eyes replaced, and now he wants it up and running. The light bulb blew the other night and his living room is pretty gloomy without it. I've promised to buy him some new ones.'

Binty nods and sips her tea. She remembers a butter-hot June day when an old woman in a pale green beret, green dress, green tights and green shoes danced alongside a jazz band outside the Musée de la Légion d'honneur in Paris. Binty watched the woman's small marionette steps; tap, tap, tap. Nearby a banjo player plucked 'When You're Smiling'.

'Wow!' Binty cried. She always thinks of the old woman as the green woman because she was green and young inside. When the band struck up 'La Vie en Rose', Dan rested his hands gently on Binty's hips and together they swayed to the music. Dan wanted her right there and then. In their room in a small Montmartre hotel, channelling the green woman's energy, Binty strutted across the richly carpeted floor while Dan with his twinkly eyes and warm smile clapped and whistled. When she stopped her ferocious jig, he knelt before her and planted delicate kisses on her flamenco feet. She felt his want. Now these very same memories flutter and lose some of their colouring, along with all the other Paris and Valencia weekends they shared.

She is brought back to the present when the woman sitting

opposite her breaks the silence and says, 'It's the morning sickness that makes it hard. I'm three months gone.' A malformed star explodes on the edge of Binty's universe.

'Just you and me, Binty,' Dan told her one day. 'No screaming brats for us, life's too short.' And Binty pushed away all images of small, pliable bodies filled with her breast milk.

'Congratulations,' she hears herself say.

'My boyfriend's happy enough, but I've had terrible heart-burn,' the woman says.

Bet you have, thinks Binty.

'I drink flat coke. It helps. Most things go bad if you leave the caps or lids off, but not coke.'

Suddenly John Legend is singing 'Written in the Stars'. The woman checks her phone and says, 'I need to take this.' Leaving the table, she begins whispering into the phone, her voice low and husky. Binty watches her stand near the toilets. She nods, smiles and blows a kiss into the mouth piece. With little mincing steps she returns to her chair.

She beams. 'There. We've kissed and made up. Said he's sorry. I know he loves me really.'

Binty says nothing.

'He does,' the woman says. Quickly she stands and says she must go, has a train to catch.

'It's not far. He'd normally take me but he suffers with migraines. He's got a killer one tonight.'

Binty knows all about Dan's migraines.

'I'm going that way,' Binty says and the women leave the Mugs and Hugs bar together.

They walk in silence with only the sounds and scratches of night around them. The woman's heels clickety-click alongside the soft pad of Binty's trainers. In different circumstances, Binty doubts they would have been friends. The woman pops open her handbag and offers her a polo mint but she says no, she hates the hole. The station platform is deserted.

'Dead quiet, isn't it?' the woman says. 'Look, you really don't have to stay with me, I'll be fine.'

'It's okay. Just wanted to see you safely onto the train. You've had a tough night.'

'What are you? A carer or something?'

'No, not me. Couldn't be a carer. I work at McKinnons.' Binty's surprised when she hears herself tell the truth.

'The brewery?'

'Yeah, Tottenham's first for over a hundred years.'

'What do you do?'

'Payroll, hiring and firing, stuff like that. Our beers take some beating, you should try them.'

'No, I'm a G and T girl. Never liked beer, it always gives me wind.'

Other passengers walk onto the platform.

'My feet are blocks of ice,' the woman remarks. Binty looks down at the woman's feet. Her scuffed black shoes suddenly seem dull and undeserving; her citrus perfume now hangs like acrid smog.

Dan has given this woman a child. He uses the four-letter word, love. He used to tell Binty love was cliché. This woman has all that Binty wants, all Binty deserves. It will take only the slightest of nudges, a quick push. 'Push, shove,' her ancestors whisper, 'as quickly as we'd wring a chicken's neck. Go on, do it. Do it. Push. Shove.' She will say that the woman lost her footing – she already tripped over earlier, didn't she?

The train charges down the track, and Binty and the woman step forward.

Binty closes her eyes. She moves forward, holds out her arms to shove the woman onto the track – but the doors slide open and the woman steps onto the train. Binty isn't sure what's happened, but the moment has gone as quickly as it arrived. She stares at the train doors closing; her heart pounds and her arms droop by her sides.

Looking curious, the woman throws her a puzzled smile and waves, hopeful and brave like a child on her first day at school. Binty steps back from the platform and tells herself to keep breathing.

It must have been something the woman said, something about little kicks inside and the hope of new life filled with warm milk. Binty was raised on farms, urban and rural. She spent endless summer holidays on her grandparents' land. The blood of farmhands and milkmaids flows in her veins, and she knows the sweet joys of lambing. As she watches the train disappear into the distance, taking with it the light bulb and the woman with the little kicks inside her, Binty remembers how goats have a way of staring long after you're gone. The farm has followed her to this very spot. It is time to let go.

XI

Olivia's Story

One of Olivia's earliest memories is of making mud pies in the back garden. The fat worms make her toes wriggle as she bores her T-bar shoes deeper into the curdled black soil.

'It's a funny thing that,' remarks Flo Sheldon, glancing through the kitchen window before she returns to the ironing. 'The way Ollie prefers dirt to her Cindy doll.'

Olivia is six years old and Peter a year older. Together they make pies that no one will eat.

Trilling like a bird, Olivia sings her favourite nursery rhyme and pretends she is riding a cock-horse to Banbury Cross. 'I'm the best singer in the whole wide world,' she adds.

'No, you're not,' Peter says, rolling his eyes.

'I am.'

'Not.'

'Am.'

'Not.'

'Am.'

Frowning, Olivia watches her small brown hands gather the earth and pat it down firmly into the bucket. Tipping the soil out, she folds it into the newspaper.

'Half a crown,' Olivia says to Peter. 'That's half a crown, please, sir.'

She receives a plastic tiddlywink in exchange for a bundle of newspaper and mud.

There's a rabbit hutch along from the kitchen door, near the corner where the brick wall bends. Uncle Tommy creeps outside with a few carrots clutched in one hand. Olivia glances over; he has one ordinary leg and one extraordinary short leg weighed down by a heavy built-up boot.

'It's to keep him steady,' her mother has explained, but Olivia doesn't understand the appeal of being weighed down. The boot reminds her of reins and being held back.

Uncle Tommy opens the rabbit hutch and forces a fat hand inside. The rabbit scurries towards the carrots and Olivia hears the insistent sound of nibbling and grinding. Uncle Tommy turns. He winks at Olivia and opens the fly to his trousers. The worm he holds is hard, pink and swollen.

Looking away, Olivia quickly buries her gaze deep in the soil. With his back to the kitchen door, Peter sings about London burning, and when the children peer over at the rabbit hutch, Uncle Tommy has disappeared inside the house.

It's Friday, fish day. Dinner is fish, chips and sweet garden peas. Flo Sheldon doesn't cook on Fridays; it's an evening off and she goes down the chippy. Olivia asks for the tomato ketchup bottle and when she isn't looking, Peter steals a chip from the dark puddle of Sarson's vinegar on her plate.

Olivia's chair backs on to a tall cupboard where Flo stores all the jars and bottles filled with materials she needs for repairing things, including the bottles of glue Olivia's mother brings back from the factory where she works. The glue factory is a big red-brick building near Tottenham Hale. Olivia knows that her mother hides more of those little glass bottles in the cramped space under the sink.

Her mother has enough glue to mend anything that breaks; teacups, doll's house furniture, vases, ornaments and her father's reading glasses. Her father needs his glasses to do the pools, and to read the newspaper and the many letters that fall through the slot in the front door.

Uncle Tommy gobbles down his food like a wolf, and Aunty Flo says, 'Manners, Tom.' He continues eating like he's not seen food in a long while, and eventually Olivia stops eating her supper altogether. She drops her spoon and doesn't want to bend down under the dinner table to pick it up; she's afraid she will look across in the dark under the table and see the strange worm.

'Pick up your spoon, love,' coaxes Aunty Flo. 'You'll need it for your pudding.'

It's jam roly-poly. Olivia likes the jam suet circles that go round and round and round. With sharp green eyes, Uncle Tommy is watching her, one hand shovelling the chips, the other beneath the table.

Scratching at her elbow, she looks across at Peter, willing him to read something in her eyes.

'It's all right, Ollie. I'll get it.' Sighing, Peter reaches down and brings the silver spoon up from the dark.

'Wash it off, Peter, there's a love,' Aunty Flo says. With her little finger she picks at her long, narrow teeth. 'That's the only problem with fish, the bloomin' bones.' Olivia's dad says Aunty Flo looks like a horse. Olivia likes horses and often pretends to be one while Peter feeds her cubes of white sugar.

Peter returns with the wet spoon, and Olivia eats her portion of jam roly-poly and custard.

'You know what'll happen if you eat too much jam roly-poly, don't you, Ollie?' Uncle Tommy asks, craning his head forward. Olivia shakes her head.

'You'll turn into a roly-poly yourself! Ha!' And he laughs out loud. His mouth breaks open like a bread bin, his teeth a cramped clatter of yellow.

Aunty Flo laughs and digs him in the side. 'Give over, you daft bugger. Don't be telling the child that, she'll go off her food. You eat up, Ollie. You need your food if you're going to be a big, strong girl.'

'Ollie doesn't need to be big and strong. She's made of sugar and spice and all things nice, aren't you, Ollie?'

Olivia is suddenly full. Her stomach heaves as if she's been eating gravel, and she throws up. The sick wets the front of her polka-dot cotton dress and douses the carpet around the legs of her chair.

'Now look what you've gone and done.' Scolding Uncle Tommy, Aunty Flo rises from her chair.

'Not to worry, poppet. Accidents happen. Come on, I'll clean you up.' Aunty Flo leads Olivia to the bathroom and her small hand disappears in her aunt's padded palm. Aunty Flo is a big woman and Olivia likes nothing better than sitting in the warm, safe valley that is her lap.

When they return, Peter has fallen asleep on the sofa, purring, his mouth open. Uncle Tommy is watching the television, guzzling crisps from a large Tupperware bowl, and Olivia's mother is waiting, her deep-brown eyes heavy and flecked with tiredness.

'She been all right, Flo?'

'Good as gold.'

'Thanks for looking after her. I'm so grateful for your help.' Aunty Flo pats Olivia's mother on the back and gives her a little squeeze.

'Don't give it another thought, love, that's what neighbours are for.'

Olivia has a nightmare that night; she wets the bed and tells her mother and father about scary worms. She misses school the following day. She says she's scared of the rabbit in the garden at the Sheldons' house and doesn't want to stay with them anymore.

Olivia's mother finds another family who can take care of her after school until she finishes her shift and can collect her. The Hicks family live at the corner of Carlingford Road and Stanmore Road, in a lofty terraced house with creaking stairs and floorboards. Mrs Hicks has strong, muscular legs and rides a bike. Patsy Hicks wears a neat bob and plays hopscotch with Olivia at school playtimes. She can balance on one leg to a count of nine. At the end of each school day Olivia goes home with Patsy and Mrs Hicks until her mother collects her.

Mrs Hicks doesn't allow any playing in the back garden or on the stairs. With thin, tight lips she says that she's the grown-up and she knows what's what. She gives Ollie the house rules and tells her that before dinner hands must be washed and grace must be said. The high-ceilinged rooms are draughty and the permanently drawn curtains block out any light. Olivia suspects that Mrs Hicks thinks wicked things might creep in from outside under cover of light. She sounds off about sinful goings-on at the Salisbury pub, the importance of keeping a clean mind and watching your Ps and Qs. Sometimes the Hicks' house feels like a church and Olivia finds herself speaking in whispers.

*

Although she's not supposed to have favourites, Barney Cheung is Olivia's favourite pupil. He plays his poetry like a violin and twists at his school tie when he's thinking. He is short-tongued and doesn't get on with his Rs, so he asks other children to read his poems. Sticking on gold stars like postage stamps, Olivia commends Barney's consistently excellent efforts.

She meets Brian while they are both shopping in the frozen vegetable aisle in Morrisons. Brian makes her laugh when he introduces himself as a frozen food fiend and attempts unsuccessfully to balance a bag of broccoli on his head. Three months into their relationship, he says, 'Never thought I'd bag me a clever bird, a teacher with a handful of ologies.' He throws his heavy arm round Olivia's shoulders; she wishes he wouldn't but she doesn't say. Her shoulders grow round beneath his weight.

They have very little furniture – a bed, a fish tank, a bean bag – and for months they go without a television or an oven, eating tinned or raw food, which Brian insists is good for them. People tell them how exciting it is, this starting out, setting up home, but Olivia doesn't feel anything is beginning; rather, things continue much the same.

At Alexandra Palace one Sunday, they fly a kite. It is a large red kite, a Chinese dragon with a long flickering tail. It skates across the blue-white sky. A fierce September wind is blowing hard and Brian says this is good and bad.

'The bloody kite. I knew this would happen.'

The kite escapes but becomes snared in the branches of a tree.

Olivia watches Brian pace around the foot of the tree, kicking at the trunk and yanking at the cord.

'Why do there need to be so many dumb trees anyway?'

'I like trees,' Olivia says and smiles up at the kite. The kite has had the guts to do what she can't.

'Stupid thing, stuff it,' Brian says and storms off. The silent bus ride home is mainly downhill. Their small flat is on Downhills Park Road and overlooks a playing field.

After she's finished marking the children's homework, Olivia stacks the blue exercise books in a tidy pile near her brown briefcase, which she keeps near the front door. She hears the sound of running bathwater; Brian always turns it aquamarine when he adds a capful of bubble bath.

He is quiet after their return from Alexandra Palace but pokes his head round the bathroom door to say, 'I didn't want to say anything and I know you'll tell me if there's anything to tell. Only I saw the box and I just wondered if...'

'Yes... Positive.'

As he shakes his head and punches the air, Olivia feels him look at her as if he's seeing her for the first time.

When the time comes it is as if every river in the world is flowing through her body, and all of them are bursting their banks. She loses track of the hours and when the small, wet body falls between her thighs, she slumps back and knows why birth and love are called labour. For a long time, she stares at the father and child.

The naming of the baby is a struggle between Henry, Dan or Jack. Olivia doesn't like Brian's suggestions of Thomas, Tom or Tommy.

'Does it make you think of a peeping Tom? Bit pervy,' he asks. Olivia doesn't answer.

'I like Dan,' she says. 'It's solid.'

'Not too desperate, then?' he laughs.

Brian sterilises the bottles, changes Dan's nappies, treats his cradle cap and tastes Olivia's breast milk. Strolling with Dan in his buggy, Olivia notes that the kite is still there in the tree, watching her life continue.

'Only children are lonely children, they have issues,' Brian says. 'Not pointing any fingers, Ollie, but it's a known thing.'

Olivia can only make love with the lights off – she doesn't like being looked at or looking – and Dan remains an only child. She has her A-level students and she squeezes good enough grades from them to send them on to university. Brian rents an allotment and grows marrows, tomatoes, squash and strawberries. The strawberries taste like petrol, but Olivia doesn't tell him this or that there is metal in the air, pollution from cars.

Brian talks less these days. She suspects that he thinks she's withholding her eggs. From behind the living-room curtains, she watches father and son plod along in slow rhythm to the allotment, heavy steps, heavy arms, hunched shoulders, continuing much the same.

*

The tears won't come when they bury Olivia's mother. They're dammed up inside her head somewhere. Although her movements are deliberate and slow, she often does things twice over.

On the day of the funeral it rains and the sky is dark, but it is the only kind of day on which her mother would have agreed to be buried.

Had it been a warm, sunny day her mother would have been sunning herself, kicking off her shoes, saying, 'Forget the grass stains, let's have a picnic.'

As she gives the eulogy in a dry, shrivelled voice, Olivia recalls memories she has long forgotten. Memories of their weekly visits to Lindy's launderette and the regular hunter-gathering for twenty-pence and fifty-pence pieces, her mother's chestnut-coloured beehive boxed backwards by the wind as she struggled with the clothes line, her wildcat temper and long-playing love for Olivia's father. At her mother's funeral, there are faces Olivia doesn't know or hasn't seen for a long time. They shake her hand, nod and offer mild, soothing words.

From the beginning Olivia's mother had found fault with her, said she was haunted.

'You think too much, Olivia. That book reading's doing you no good. It's giving you notions.'

Notions and ideas were dangerous things; they could make you take flight and forget yourself.

When she was thirty years old, shortly after Dan's birth, Olivia visited her mother, told her about Uncle Tommy. Uncle Tommy, who sat in her pocket like a bunch of keys tearing away at the lining.

'Well, you can hardly call that abuse, can you? I mean, he didn't touch you or nothing,' her mother said, twiddling with the buttons of her cardigan.

When Uncle Tommy died, her mother sent a wreath and

cried for most of the day. Olivia didn't attend the funeral. Her limbs didn't work that morning.

'You should have gone, Ollie. Your Aunty Flo thinks the world of you. You read too much into things, always did.'

A month after her mother's funeral, Brian leaves, this time for good. He says that he has had enough of pretending and that Dan is almost a full-grown man, he'll understand. Olivia is struck by the small suitcase he's taken and realises he has somewhere to go, someone waiting for him.

Without turning back, Brian walks down the garden path. He leaves the family car and climbs into a waiting minicab. Olivia spends many nights talking with Dan, trying to help him understand, but he doesn't.

On Monday, Olivia has the front door locks changed. Removing the fridge magnets that Brian thought very funny, she feels expansion and freedom, like she's thrown off an outgrown girdle. After Olivia was born her mother invested in a Playtex Cross-Your-Heart bra and girdle and although she said the girdle crushed her ribs, she declared it a lifeline.

Unable to tread down the rush of gladness beginning at her fingertips, Olivia cancels the subscription to sports television and finds herself humming. This is a new kind of breathing, a genuine starting out.

*

Olivia allows the staff to bathe her and brush her teeth. They wonder at the surprising whiteness of her teeth and the meek splendour of the tight curls she's warred with for much of her life. Among the staff at Belleview Care Home are Maggie, the Irish cook, Babsy, the Trinidadian staff leader, and a few women from Poland who do the other shifts. Olivia finds that most homes for older people smell of damp and things decomposing, but Belleview is very clean.

Dan spent a lot of time searching for a residential home where his mother would be happy. And Olivia is very happy. The house is big and double-fronted with a large plot of land where she has her own herb garden. She has made friends with Seb, the teenager who lives in the house whose garden backs onto the Belleview. There's something broken in Seb's eyes, the same wreckage she used to see in Dan's eyes when he was a teenager.

Olivia makes two friends amongst the other residents: Henryk and Gwendoline.

Olivia's room is L-shaped with bay windows that look onto the back garden. Dan pays extra for the view. She has sight of a pear tree that each year is jewelled with pendulous fruit and a dazzling azalea bush with gaudy magenta blooms, but it is the regular bars of soap placed in her bathroom that thrill her. Like duck eggs of cool marbled beauty they sit meekly on the bathroom sink until water spoils their purity and perfection. The staff assume that Olivia dislikes washing, unaware of her love of symmetry, but Henryk understands.

Henryk is Swiss and used to be a professional opera singer. He describes himself as an artist. Olivia notes the exact Windsor knots of his loud, flashy ties and ignores the worn cuffs. It tickles Olivia when Henryk throws back his head and yodels. He reminds her of Frank Ifield but Henryk hasn't heard of Frank Ifield and nor has anyone else in the home; she feels very old and foolish for mentioning his name.

'It doesn't matter whether anyone has or hasn't heard of

your Frank Ifield, Ollie. He's known to you and that's all that matters,' Henryk says. He tidies up Olivia's muddles. He could have said, 'Whatever,' and dismissed her worries by yawning, changing the subject, closing a drawer, turning a key or doing whatever it is that smug and uncaring people do when things don't matter to them – but he doesn't.

Gwendoline steals things from other people's rooms, anything bright, and hides her growing, glittering loot under her bed. The staff find money taken from the Monopoly bank along with a garlic press and nail clippers. Thinking she is eight years old again, she spends many afternoons roaming Belleview searching for her long-dead sister in a private game of hide-and-seek.

From time to time, windows of coherence and clarity suddenly squirm open, and Olivia discovers that Gwendoline was once an investigative journalist, covering war zones. Everybody in the care home used to be somebody else.

Throughout the day another resident, Hilda Roe, brays like a mule. She bawls, 'I don't belong here, take me home. I want to go home.' At the breakfast table Hilda tips over her white china plate of hard-boiled eggs and buttered toast and asks Iga, one of the Polish care assistants, 'Why didn't he say he loved me?' Iga shakes her head. It is Hilda's daughter, Cupcake, who explains to Iga and Olivia what her mother means: 'Mum's talking about my dad. She's always talking about him.'

Cupcake visits daily and often reads to Hilda from a small black leather bible. Hilda sits silently, unmoving, until one afternoon, she cries, 'Stop, stop... I don't like this. You sound like the Grim Reaper and I'm not ready to meet my maker.' And she crumbles into a shawled pile of sobs. Hilda stays at

Belleview for a further two weeks until Cupcake wheels her out of the house and down the ramp for the last time.

All the residents wave and say goodbye; it's almost like a royal procession, but Hilda, like a horse in blinkers, looks straight ahead and through each and every one of them as if they aren't there and never have been.

There are activities: reminiscence Mondays, bingo on Tuesdays, yoga and stretching on Wednesdays and Cluedo, Dominoes and Monopoly on Thursdays. Although the staff can't be sure, newly arrived Dexter seems to have swallowed a domino; the double six is missing and Dexter has a habit of eating small, immobile objects. Olivia wins – it's Colonel Mustard in the library with the lead piping. She shines brightly.

In a quiet corner of the lounge near the bookcases filled with board games and books, Henryk whispers, 'Everyone says I'm in denial about growing old but how else do I survive it if I don't deny it?'

'You could accept it.'

Cupping her face between his hands, Henryk says, 'Ah, sadly, Olivia, I have neither your sagacity nor your grace.' And after kissing her on her forehead, he clears his throat and climbs up the scales, beginning with do-re-mi.

On Fridays it's Singalong with Babsy and on Saturday afternoons children from the local Seventh-Day Adventist church visit and read to the residents. Olivia sees herself in Pearl, the watchful, moon-faced child who likes to read Bible stories to her on Saturdays. She wears, thick-rimmed glasses and observes Olivia closely with curious, sharp eyes. Pearl asks Olivia questions like 'Why do you live here?', 'How old are you?', 'Do your wrinkles hurt?', 'Do you know what recycling means?', and 'What is the best day you've ever had?' On Sundays, Dan visits with his new wife Femi (whom Olivia privately calls 'frosty Femi') and their perfect infant son Benjamin. Sometimes she wonders what became of Binty – she liked Binty, a caring, reliable woman.

Olivia thinks of Pearl's question about her best days; those when as a child she played with Peter in the back garden, and her wedding day when she danced until her feet were blistered. Her very best day was the day before yesterday, when Henryk held her and told her that she was the love of his life.

It's true what people say about life flashing past. Like dew, memories pour down, sights, sounds, scents, tastes and touch, until Olivia finds herself somewhere near the beginning. Her last memory is of making mud pies, her small fingers earthed, her T-bar shoes boring deep into curdled black soil. London's burning, rings on her fingers, bells on her toes. Am. Am. Am.

XII

Seb's Story

There isn't any special occasion for the barbecue party other than this being yet another attempt to fill an empty Sunday afternoon in a long line of empty Sunday summer afternoons. Seb and Paula drape lazily in striped green and white deckchairs. On the far side of the carefully mown garden lawn, Seb's mother Gina serves glasses of white wine from a round silver tray. A sparkling smile lights her summer-flushed face, revealing small, uneven teeth, as Paula's father Des takes a wine-filled glass.

'Do they seriously think no one knows?' Seb asks.

'Your mum and my dad? It's a joke, isn't it?' Paula says.

'No. Not really.' Seb stuffs a handful of Wotsits into his mouth.

He watches his mother, red with heat and sangria, tiptoe back inside the house through the open French doors.

'Weird, really. I mean, it's like my dad's got two wives.' Paula picks at a scab on her knee. 'He's got my mum, although they've kind of split up, and he's got your mum on the side. He'd be better off in Utah or Lagos. Abiola says a lot of men have more than one wife in Nigeria, it's no big deal.'

'Don't be stupid, Paula. Your dad's an arsehole and my mum's a drunk.'

'Well, it cuts both ways. In a way your mum's got two husbands: your dad, who isn't an arsehole, and my dad, who is.' Paula pushes her straight blonde hair away from her face.

Seb shrugs. 'Whatever.'

Seb and Paula have been friends since primary school. They sit with their backs to the sun, watching the adults. In the garden there is wisteria, magnolia, honeysuckle, clematis and an ornamental pond, home to Koi carp, glistering like slithers of gold and silver foil in the water.

A spindly buddleia shrub is tucked in the corner; this is also the kind of garden that tempts butterflies. There are thick shards of jagged glass on the tops of the walls to keep out cats but you can't stop birds from chirping. Seb knows birds chirp whenever they want to; birdsong can't be altered by walls or broken glass. Olivia, who was a resident of the Belleview care home, used to talk with him about birds, shrubs and mystical things.

'No, I'm not frightened of death,' she once told him. 'It's the way of all living things. Do you know, there is a very special tree – I can't remember its name but each year on the same day and at exactly the same time all its leaves fall off. Now isn't that something?' Hunting through the internet, Seb tried to find the name of the tree but never did. Olivia died last month but he remembers watching her careful movements as she planted plugs of bright pink lobelia into the flower beds and sprinkled black sunflower hearts and white millet onto the bird feeder stand. Once her gardener-gloved hands reached up over the garden wall and handed him a single fragrant yellow rose. Its heavy head toppled forward.

'This one's for friendship,' Olivia said. 'When I was a child, Seb, I spent hours in the back garden making mud pies. Ha. Now that was a very long time ago – a lifetime ago.' Her face gleamed and brightened like it had sucked in all the sun.

'Do you know First Nations people used lobelia to treat coughs and colds? There's a herbal remedy for every sickness known to man, Seb. Every sickness.'

Wearing a wide-brimmed straw hat and kneeling on a small mat, Olivia dug away at the earth with her trowel. Furiously she snipped at the branches of wisteria that clambered over the fence from Seb's garden into the back garden of the Belleview.

'Even beautiful things have to be cut back,' she told Seb as she stuffed the branches into a green bin liner. 'It'll all be recycled anyway. They'll turn it into compost or mulch – nothing goes to waste these days.' Seb misses her. She made him feel as if he was wrapped up in a cosy duvet. He used to smile as she talked about the joys of kite flying and the power of sleep.

When not talking about their parents, Seb and Paula try to estimate how many people get killed each year by flying golf balls or falling coconuts, how many people kill the wrong person and not the one they intend to kill, and how many people kill but don't intend to kill at all. Paula talks about Mr Bromsgrove, the maths teacher, complaining that he smells of tobacco and sweat. And Seb talks about the music teacher, Miss 'Massive-Bum' Oleander, who stands too close.

'Latest news flash,' Paula blurts, 'is Elaine Grant has been swallowing molly like Haribos in the girls' toilets.' And Seb tells Paula about Shane Pritchard in 12J with the haunted phone.

'Liar,' Paula says, squinting her sky-grey eyes.

'Shane's phone used to belong to some dead guy who got stabbed at a party over in Hackney. I kid you not.'

'When I go to uni next year I hope my conversations will be more… enlightened.'

'Oh, Paula, you should hear yourself sometimes.'

'I mean, haunted phones, really?'

'Most of the time all you and your friends talk about is guys – not exactly intellectually challenging.'

'We don't talk about all guys, just black guys. Most girls prefer black guys – I mean, it's kind of uncool to be white now. You do know that, don't you?'

'Maybe, maybe not. It's kind of messed up though, to be cool or uncool just because of the skin you're in.' Seb shrugs and drags his fingers through his mop of bushy hair.

'Black guys are free of all that entitlement stuff. Privilege spoils people. I mean, look at my dad,' Paula says, screwing up her face against the fierce rays of the sun. 'My eyes are watering. I should have worn my Ray-Bans,' she moans.

'You're kidding? You got Ray-Bans?' Seb's eyes widen.

'Yep, well… sort of. Primark lookalike Ray-Bans.'

'Of course, Primark equivalents. Ha. A lot of guys don't like brainy girls like you, but I'm cool, I like all the big words and weird ideas.'

'Oh, shut up, Seb!' Paula laughs and throws a handful of popcorn at him.

Seb's attention shifts. 'Look, there she is, the goddess.' Leaning over, he pokes Paula in the side. The Dukes have arrived; Mr and Mrs Ben and Lacey Duke. Dainty Lacey Duke resembles a fairy and walks on grass like it's newly fallen snow. She's barefoot. Her maxi dress is covered in a pattern of small meadow flowers, matching the crown of plastic daisies resting on her head. Lacey Duke takes care of sick animals at the local animal shelter.

Ben, her husband, towers over her, closing in on her like a great bear, but when he grins he's buck-toothed and goofy.

Paula and Seb fall about laughing. Paula pulls a face. 'Gross or what? She's like all Princess Perfect, everything I want to be, and he's Frankenstein monster man. What does she see in him?' Paula sucks fizzy pink lemonade through a long straw.

'That's easy – Ben's a nice person,' says Seb.

Lacey Duke walks over and, greeting Seb and Paula, asks them about their school holidays. When she returns to the patio, they decide that she smells of apple blossom or how they think apple blossom should smell. They can hear the beginnings and drizzled-down ends of conversations. Seb's father Mike sits apart, looking down at a sandwich in the centre of a small paper plate, his face bolted like a barn door.

'Do you think we'll mess up when we're older?' Seb asks, studying his father's face.

'Probably. Looks like that's all adults do, and then they get dementia and die.'

Seb turns round and stares at Paula. 'God, you're cheerful.'

Seb's mother Gina kicks off her strappy white sandals and runs barefoot from the patio onto the lawn.

'Come on, turn the music up. Let's dance,' she calls out, waving her arms. Paul Simon sings about being someone's bodyguard, and Mike rubs away at his jaw, staring down at the grass.

'Oh no, not another golden oldie,' Paula says and shakes her head. 'I hate this dead music.'

'Anyone want to dance?' Gina shouts and Mike slowly

stands, his heavy frame awkward, and walks towards her. A frown crosses her face, but she takes her husband's hand anyway.

'There's no need to hold me,' she says between gritted teeth and shifts his hands from her waist. 'Anyway, it's too hot for that,' she adds. After a short while she pulls away, rubs her forehead and says she needs another drink.

She used to spend a lot of time dusting, polishing, wiping and vacuuming. When Zak Katz from 12F visited, she insisted he remove his shoes. New carpet, she explained. After Zak left, Gina grumbled that she could smell dog crap and went from room to room with carpet freshener and a disinfectant-soaked J-cloth.

The only time Seb can remember Gina coming alive was when she spoke about the time before he was born when she and Mike motorbiked across North America and visited the Hotel California in Mexico. She said the staff in the gift shop played the Eagles track over and over, but even after she left the store she couldn't turn the song off – it was like a squirrel in her head. The Hotel California is built on the Tropic of Cancer. Gina told Seb this was significant; she said the circle couldn't stay still, it continually drifted southwards and dragged the Hotel California with it. Cruising along the Californian coast, Mike and Gina stopped in Santa Barbara. They strolled hand-in-hand along sunny State Street where city brides spilled from the county courthouse offices like giddy taffeta ghosts.

Gina said she'd never got over the abruptness of things changing, said she had no time to prepare.

'Women have to deal with loss all the days of their lives,' she told him. 'Loss pulls you down, catches you unawares – but you're a man, Seb, you'll never have to worry about women's stuff. The way we live now, it goes against the seasons.'

Late last year Gina stopped doing the housework. Dust gathered and grubby laundry tumbled over the Ali-Baba basket. Missing kitchen knives went unnoticed, and Seb watched his mother reroute her attention from her home to her hair, make-up and nails. She had her eyebrows threaded, cultivated celebrity arches and transformed herself from mouse brown to Marilyn Monroe blonde. Gazing into her dressing-table mirror, she constantly monitored her changing reflection. A beautiful face is one without surprises, she told Seb; she was considering a nose job.

He noticed the stiff silence stalking the house, lurking between chairs and tables, hiding behind doors and refusing conversation. Complaining that the house was too warm, Gina kept leaving the living room and bedroom windows open. She said she wanted to move, to leave Tottenham. She hated the area, said it had gone down, was dangerous, that Seb could and then that Seb would get stabbed if they didn't move. Mike shook his head, said there were far worse places than Tottenham. He closed the windows quietly behind her and reminded both Seb and Gina that leaving windows open was a security risk. Gina served up lukewarm dinners, frequently didn't finish sentences and regularly lost or forgot things. Her car keys. Her door keys. Her phone. Her purse. The time. Where she'd been. Mike retreated into the garden shed, said he was busy fixing things, but all Seb heard was his father pulling things apart.

A lost scarf was found balled up under the driver's seat of the family car. At first glance it looked like a blood-soaked rag. It was a twenty-first birthday present given to Gina by her mother.

Gina called it her Lady Macbeth scarf. As she carefully folded it away in her handbag, she said to Mike, 'Why is it so hard for you to see that I'm trying to replace all the things I've lost and holding on to those things I'm losing?' Mike told her he understood but she shook her head and said he didn't and never would.

Seb hates holding all this adult stuff. Their words live in his head and he quietens their noise by losing himself in Xbox games where invincible immortals conquer arctic wastelands and vanquish saber-toothed, two-headed beasts.

Gina's body softens when Des is about. She laughs too loudly at his unfunny jokes; her tight mouth slackens and twitches, like she's about to pounce or be pounced on.

Twirling around and lifting a glass to the canvas of big blue sky, Gina asks no one in particular, 'Can you divorce someone on the grounds of broken promises?' She looks over at Mike; his eyes are on a rhododendron. The guests don't seem to hear and carry on their commentary about what a good summer it has been.

'She's drunk,' Seb mutters and Paula nods, draining her glass of lemonade.

Gina continues, her voice an unsteady drawl, 'I mean, it can't be right that someone promises you one thing, one life, that they're gonna be somebody, that you're gonna be some-body, and all they ever become is what they already were. What do you call that, fraud? Failure to launch? It's got to have a name. It's like being cheated – it is being cheated. They used to call it a breach of promise. And there was a remedy back then, wasn't there? You'd take out a heart-balm lawsuit and everything would be put right. It's just common sense, you can take your clothes back if there's a flaw or something and they give you back your money. A refund.'

She drinks her glass of sangria in two big gulps and stares down at the pond, at the glittering bodies of Koi carp.

'Look at all those coins,' she says, pointing at the pond and the pennies that lie at the bottom. 'Does anyone remember throwing a coin in the pond and being visited by Lady Luck? Anyone?'

Swinging round, she looks at her guests, who are chattering among themselves.

'The Koi don't look bothered, do they?' She starts laughing and tearing off clumps of bread from a baguette. The guests stop talking and watch as Gina throws lumps of bread into the water. Ripping the baguette, she shouts, 'Let them eat cake! Let them eat cake!'

The Koi scatter and Mike bends down to scoop out the soggy lumps.

'No,' Gina shouts, 'you leave that bread alone, you bloody well leave it there. All of it. They're my fucking wishes, not yours.'

In a quieter voice, as if talking to herself, she adds, 'They'll survive. Everyone knows Koi are strong – they swim against the current.'

She turns and hurries towards the kitchen. Raising her voice, she says, 'Let's keep it merry, folks. More corn on the cob coming up.'

Mike is a quiet man with gentle lines and no corners. He tends to the garden, cuts away at the weeds, but they seem to ignore his efforts and return again and again. Ground elder, Mike tells Seb, is the worst kind.

The chatter bubbles up and Paula's father Des says to Ben Duke, 'Most high roads in this country have got a terminal illness. Even Curry's has closed down, and Tottenham isn't exactly a field of dreams.'

'Well, we think a bookshop on the High Road is just what the area needs. We'll have a weekly reading group, a supplementary school at the weekends and a café. We've got to dream big,' says Ben Duke.

'Build it and they will come,' Lacey says dreamily, stroking her husband's face.

'Yep, build it and they will come,' Ben echoes.

'Ha.' Des downs his can of beer. 'Who are you now, Kevin Costner?'

'There are lots of good people in Tottenham, doing good things and trying to make it a good place for everyone who lives here. A bookshop is just a small part of it.'

'Well, I'm all for progress. Good luck to you, Ben. I hope it all works out.' Des flips open the top buttons of his shirt, where a bunch of greying white hairs nestle like a small rodent.

Gina emerges through the French doors and, clapping her hands, hollers, 'It seems to me Tottenham's definitely going up in the world – raise your glasses, everyone! Koi carp, coins and a bookshop. Here's to bloody gentrification, people!'

There are a few bouts of laughter.

Ben Duke starts to say, 'But it's not about gentrification, it's about—'

Gina turns up the volume of the music and Ben Duke's words are drowned. Lacey pats his hand and shakes her head. 'Let it go,' she whispers.

'Okay, let's keep it light and happy, people,' Gina says loudly. 'This is a party, after all; no politics and no doom and gloom.'

Ed Sheeran sings 'Shape of You' and a few couples start dancing. Mike smiles at his son but for Seb it's the smile of a drowning man.

'We need to keep the music down,' says Mike, pointing over the garden wall at the Belleview care home.

'Of course, we mustn't forget the old folk,' sniggers Gina, placing an unsteady finger over her lips. 'Let's play dead instead, shall we?' And she does a zombie stagger that's interrupted when she stumbles into a table.

'You need to sit down, you've had too much sun,' Mike says and tries to steer her towards a large wicker chair, but she wrangles free and attempts to steady herself.

One evening when they were sitting in the living room, half-watching an old black-and-white gangster movie, Mike told Seb that his mother came from a long line of remarkable women and men whose thinking changed and gave way in later life, like shelves in a bookcase. He explained that it wasn't Gina's fault; growing older was sometimes hard for people.

Seb remembers when Grandad Henry, his mother's father, got older he began to put everything and everyone into numbers. He used to shout about terrible twos. That one's got the dark thirteen about him. Oh, there goes a legs eleven. All at sixes and sevens. Seb was almost pleased when worsening health quietened his grandad's bingo tongue and timid shy smiles replaced the boxes into which he put people.

The air is now thick with hickory and burgers but Lacey Duke shakes her head and continues nibbling on a cheese and sea salt cracker.

'She's turned vegetarian,' Paula says. 'And she's joined Extinction Rebellion.'

Lacey Duke explains that meat is bad for babies, makes them aggressive; she gently rubs the mound of her round stomach. Adele belts out 'Rumour Has It' and Ben Duke covers his wife's shoulders with sun protection cream, his big hands growing small with tenderness.

Pulling a face of disgust, Paula removes slices of grilled tomato from her burger bun. 'Yuck,' she says. 'You know, one of my aunts loves tomatoes. She actually puts sugar on them.'

'Which aunt?'

'Aunty Lulu. The sexy one.'

'The one who had three husbands?'

'No, four.'

Picking up a tray, Gina hands out glasses of fruit-filled Pimm's. The front of her tight-fitting, zip front dress is stained red with dried wine spills.

'Why isn't everybody drinking?' Gina coos. 'Come on – Ken? Nyoka? Abdul? Is this a party or is this a party?'

Slouching in the deckchair, Seb looks on, but sits up when Gina, putting down the tray, stops like she's remembered something and darts back inside the house.

'You should go see that she's all right,' Paula says. Wearily, Seb stands.

The ketchup on Seb's chin could have been blood. Last term he stopped Janusz Kowalczyk taking dinner money from some Somalian boys in Year Seven. Sometimes Seb finds it has to be more than words, more than threats. When Seb came home that day he dumped his bloodied school shirt in the washing machine. Although Gina never asked any questions, he wishes she had.

Des's eyes follow Gina inside the house and Seb's fists ball in his pockets, the grass crisp and hard beneath his trainers. Des is about to stand, about to follow her into the house. He is so different from Seb's father. Des works as an executive for a North Sea oil company, travelling around the world.

Seb knows that with predators most things are staged and planned. Timing is everything.

A year ago, Seb and Mike used to watch *Match of the Day* together while his mother had early nights. Come on you Spurs. Shoot, shoot. Jammy Arsenal. Mike is the same man who taught him about tackling and defending. Gina is the same woman who sang about the wheels on the bus. Yet both are long gone.

Seb spits on the grass, drops the remains of his burger in a nearby bin. He can't remember his father ever raising his voice to him, let alone a hand or a fist, but Seb's fists turn to stone in his pockets. He isn't aware of walking over to the clump of tables and chairs on the patio. It is only when Paula screams and Des staggers backwards that Seb feels the kitchen knife fall from his hand and clatter to the ground.

XIII

Zu Zu's Story

Zu Zu has been driving through south-east London for the past two hours, taking once-familiar back roads and finding the landscape so changed she gets lost and is displaced, a visitor in a new land. Peckham. The Elephant. Charlie Chaplin Mile. These places once marked her youth and her flight southwards from Tottenham many years ago. She feels it is wrong that her surroundings have changed without her knowledge or consent, and her hands tighten on the steering wheel.

'Bollocks,' she says and stops fiddling with the satnav, driving on with no clear destination in mind.

She can demand that they return her children. Johnny and Frankie. The boy with the summer smile and the girl with spongy candyfloss hair who suddenly refused to talk. Frankie would only communicate with adults through the tiniest movements of her feet; little shuffles, slight surreptitious steps, easily missed. Selective Mutism, the Child and Adolescent Mental Health Services decided. One step back meant no. One step forward meant yes. To the left – maybe. To the right – play. Heel – eat. Toe – drink. Her brother Johnny described it as Frankie 'talking Pixie again'. Frankie taking pixie steps. Zu

Zu's two young children, gone. Johnny and Frankie. Five years ago today. She can't call it theft or kidnapping. The children were described by Social Services as 'failing to thrive'. Their developmental needs were not being met and their health and well-being were at risk. 'Shitty, smelly little things,' the kindly neighbours said. She was told that Mrs Widdicombe with the twitching curtains had phoned Social Services to report the condition of the home and the poor level of supervision given to the children. Day after day the kids had gone to school leaving their inebriated mother behind, who was much too drunk to know which day of the week it was.

The documents and reports read that according to concerned neighbours, Zu Zu was an 'arse-upwards mum', though 'her heart was in the right place, poor cow'. Right now, her heart rattles and flounders in the pit of her stomach. She pulls over into a quiet cul-de-sac and lights another cigarette.

Once there was Kenny, Kenny from Broadwater Farm. Kenny, her husband, with teeth as white as foam and a smile that slid, stretched and stole round the corner. He was so alive before his car hit a lamp post turning his body to a battered, lifeless mess. It was after his death that Zu Zu stumbled, her life shattering into a mosaic of a million pieces. But she found something blurring in ever-increasing drinks and in the company of non-judgemental gin devils that only she could see. They waited at the foot of her bed when she woke up and were there last thing at night, sitting beside her on the sofa. She would often sit alone at a table in the Cart Overthrown pub, drinking herself to sleep. When she walked over to the bar the Joe, the bartender, would ask her, 'All right, Zu Zu?' but she never answered because any answer would confirm that she was there and her being there meant she was far from all right.

After their dad's death, the children stuck to Zu Zu like iron filings to a bar magnet. They would hold a mirror to her mouth checking for breath and vapour, bending over her with wide eyes.

'She's breathing.'

'She's not.'

'I am,' Zu Zu would sigh, opening her eyes and ending their verbal combat.

She was told it was for the best that her children, seven-year-old Johnny and five-year-old Frankie, were placed with long-term foster carers who would take proper care of them. Zu Zu was not fit for purpose.

She can drive to the Social Services district office right now, leave her car in the parking bay at Goose Green, march straight into the reception area and demand her children's return. By showing them reports and letters she will convince them of her clean bill of health, prove that she is able and worthy, that she hasn't touched alcohol for three long years. She has a full-time job and a clean, tidy home. She hasn't stopped being a mum just because she no longer lives with her children and hasn't seen them in five years. Social Services allow 'indirect contact' and she has sent cards, gifts and letters, but it's always felt as if the authorities lopped off her limbs the day they took her children away.

H, her counsellor at the rehabilitation unit, explained that Zu Zu had experienced a traumatic and dysfunctional childhood. She told him everything. H was a softly-spoken man with the face of a clever leprechaun. No one used full names at the unit, just initials. Something about confidentiality. Zu Zu became Z. Zed. She preferred Zed to Zu Zu, which has always reminded her of the stink of the Elephant House at Regent's Park Zoo and brought back unhappy memories of school days. Zu Zu rhymes with poo poo, as

David Connell, the class bully, told everyone. She was named after her grandmother Zelda – Zu Zu had been her nickname.

She was born in Tottenham, close to Tottenham Marshes. Her childhood home was in the middle of a long, swinging arm of a road. Her best friends were Veronica Walton at number eight and Daphne Patterson at number thirty-one. Veronica's black ponytail swung behind her like a windscreen wiper, and Daphne organised regular kiss-chases that included her imaginary friend, Milo.

Daphne's parents had the front of their house crazy-paved and everyone in the street came to admire the funny tiles while Daphne's mum and dad answered questions and pointed out special touches. Daphne's parents were from Barbados and curled their Rs when they talked, even adding Rs to words when there weren't any. Zu Zu thought they sounded like pirates.

'It will stand good in all weathers,' Daphne's dad Tyrone said, standing on the garden path, a cup of coffee in his hand.

'Really? What about the colour? Doesn't that fade?' Jack Goddard from number twenty-four asked.

'No,' Daphne's mum Edna said. 'And if it does we'll get it touched up. Everyone's doing it now.' She looked at Jack Goddard, who avoided her gaze and said that he had best be getting on. Edna was a tight-lipped woman. She was a bus conductor, rarely out of uniform and never short-changed.

Zu Zu and her family lived at number sixty-four; their house sat in the middle of the road, near the traffic lights. The road flooded reliably every April, and every April they were unprepared. Zu Zu, Veronica and Daphne would dance in the dark grey floodwaters until sharp slaps to the sides of their heads brought them back to their senses and to the grown-up gravity of the situation.

She remembers her parents and all their neighbours lugging countless buckets of water from their homes. Zu Zu's mum was a short, fluffy woman with a head full of constant cold. Zu Zu once overheard her mum tell her Aunty Sue, 'I swear, Sue, that man's name goes through my bones like the word "Clacton" on a stick of rock.'

'Will you get that?' Aunty Sue said, shaking her head and rattling blonde curls. Aunty Sue said, 'Will you get that?' about most things. At the time Zu Zu shuddered. She wondered what her dad had done to fix his name to her mum's bones and whether this was part of the secret thing that went on behind their closed bedroom door from where the strange sounds came.

Zu Zu's dad was a local hardman. When he came home, he was like a big, sulky cloud and everyone tiptoed around him, but when Zu Zu was down in the mouth, her mum continually asked if a cat had got her tongue. When people, normally men, visited their home, her dad took them into the front room and the door was firmly shut behind them.

'Now you keep away from the front room and stay here in the back with me. Your dad is seeing to business,' her mum would say. Zu Zu's mum's face was always knitted with worry but set firmly like yesterday's jelly.

'Zu Zu's dad's a hitman. A hitman. A hitman. A gangster. A murderer. A hitman. Na, na, na, na, na, na, na! Zu Zu's dad's a dead man. A dead man.' David Connell and Gary Levy chanted the words over and over until their taunts drove Zu Zu into the toilets, where she was found crying by her form teacher, Ms Davies.

In the evening in a shaky voice she asked her mum, 'Is Daddy a hitman? Does he kill people?'

Her mum struck her across the face so hard that Zu Zu fell against the formica dining table and landed on the floor. Slowly and silently her mum undid the strings of her apron and turned to a pile of freshly washed clothes and linen waiting to be ironed.

From a nearby cupboard she took out a blue-white box of Robin starch and tipped the white powder into a small bowl, where she mixed the starch with water until it turned into a thin paste. Zu Zu rubbed her cheek as hot tears fell down her face.

'Now don't you ever ask such questions about your dad again, or ever question what he does or doesn't do. No matter what anyone says, no matter what you see or hear, you're not to say a word. He's your dad, for good or bad, and he's the reason we have a roof over our heads.'

She didn't face her daughter while she spoke and later Zu Zu would remember the many times throughout her life when her mum had talked to her with her back turned.

In a hidden slot of the sideboard there were fat rolls of money. The doorbell would sometimes ring late at night and if Zu Zu was awake her mum would tell her to hush and be still. Zu Zu's mum often visited the doctor and complained of tingling down one side, tiny black dots dancing before her eyes, numbness in her wrists and ringing in her ears. Every now and then she enjoyed what she called 'little tipples'. And then a little tipple too often. She hid bottles of cider in the bottom of the broom cupboard and in the rubber plant stand, and after her tipples Zu Zu saw her rinse her mouth out with 'Evening in Paris' perfume. The aches and pains concluded their form in a very aggressive cancer. Zu Zu's mum died in her sixty-fifth year; her dad died a year later. In the hospital ward, her mother's body whittled down to bone and thin grey flesh. The day before her mum died, Zu Zu sat beside her bed. Her dad left them alone while he went to stretch his legs. Zu Zu hadn't seen her parents for years; she kept a distance between herself and them.

'You shouldn't be too hard on us, Zu Zu,' her mum said.

Zu Zu looked down at her mum's face on the pillow, drawn and heavily lined.

'I'm here, Mum,' she said.

Sitting back in the driver's seat, Zu Zu lowers the window. She glances at her watch – she's normally at work at this time but she's got the day off. She remembers her first job.

'You best have your wits about you,' her mum had said.

'I will,' Zu Zu promised and yanked the zip of her anorak.

'Mr Oldfield could have given that job to anybody, but he chose you,' her mum said. 'The ad said "paper boy".'

Zu Zu had got the job and become a paper girl.

Paperboy wanted to deliver
newspapers to local addresses.
Must be reliable.
Good pay.
Any queries talk to Mr
Oldfield.

The *Daily Mirror* was most people's regular, and Zu Zu quickly learned to bend newspapers and wedge them through letterboxes, her fingers escaping the bite of tight metal flaps. She started at the top of Park Hill Road, near the corner pet shop from which pink-eyed white mice regularly escaped. The Oluwoles lived at number 192 and cooked fufu and jollof rice, their savoury aromas drifting down the road on Sundays.

The O'Donnells lived at number twelve. Mrs O'Donnell took in washing for other people. Her whites were famous for being whiter than white.

The two halves of the road were separated from one another by a bend which prevented one half of the road from seeing the other. Large Alpington House marked the bend. This maroon-coloured house stood tall and magisterial. It was a house of horror for Zu Zu because it was the home of a vicious little terrier named Lady. Lady would bark and bite, ripping the *Daily Mirror* to shreds. As soon as Zu Zu had delivered the paper, she would run down the garden path, dragging the heavy gate behind her.

Beside Alpington House there were four prefabs called Albion Villas. They were tumbledown buildings where the blue legs of wet jeans and the white arms of wet shirts were left to dry in the sun, dangling against windows. Zu Zu knew most of the road's residents. They were in and out of one another's houses, always borrowing or lending salt, tea and sugar, and swapping well-thumbed gossip.

'Have you heard about Minnie and Stevie French?' Joyce Bannister asked Zu Zu's mum. Joyce had a head full of pink plastic curlers, and wore false teeth that were too big for her small mouth.

'No, what's happened?' Zu Zu's mum asked. She was making gravy.

'What hasn't happened, more like,' Joyce whispered, folding her arms.

Zu Zu's mum stopped stirring, turned and looked at Joyce. 'For the love of Ada, are you going to tell me what's happened to Minnie and Stevie or not?'

'Well, I'm not one for gossip, but they only went and brought home the wrong baby from the hospital. Had the baby a full two weeks before they twigged, and there was everyone saying what a beautiful angel it was. I knew it could never have been theirs – too good-looking by half.'

'Have they got the right baby now?'

'Yes, plain as porridge. Minnie's doctor has put her on Valium to help her get over the shock.' Joyce sniffed and gulped down her Tetley's tea.

Zu Zu heard all the stories, except the ones that were mouthed because of her little ears.

She always took as long as she could delivering the news-paper to number 122. Walking along the front path, she'd glance in through the curtains. The boy she loved lived at 122; occasionally she glimpsed him, just a brush of body. Bobby Singh. If she was spotted, his younger brother Curtis would call out, 'Four eyes! Four eyes!' which didn't make any sense to Zu Zu because she didn't wear glasses.

At number ninety-eight lived a boy called Ivan. He was from Grenada. His parents told Zu Zu's mum they used to live in St George's, the capital. Plucky Ivan stood like a cockerel, tilted awkwardly on two left feet. He wore special 'correctional' boots, Zu Zu's mum explained. They were bluish-grey, tightly laced surgical boots that seemed punitive, as if Ivan were to blame for his difference. Zu Zu's mum said that the boots would set his feet right, that somehow they would teach his feet to unbend the wrong way and bend more correctly to the right.

As Zu Zu looks through the car window now, she remembers Ivan and hopes that later in life he has found a right-footed partner who balances him so that they walk evenly together.

'You can't go looking for yourself in somebody else, Z. It's when we go looking for ourselves in other people that we get lost. You don't need external validation,' H once said. As he spoke, the tips of his fingers met and pressed together in an arch as if he was moulding an imaginary brain – Zu Zu's brain.

At number ninety-two lived Alice Munsford and her three sisters. Other people walked but Alice Munsford floated, all lingerie and nylon-pale skin. Each time Zu Zu delivered a newspaper to the Munsfords', a gas man or an electricity man or a milkman was just leaving or about to check the gas or electric meter or deliver milk. Alice would smile with her huge, mascaraed eyes and tweet, 'And how's my darling little Zu Zu, and that very handsome dad of yours?'

The 'Avon Calling' lady, Lucinda Hancock, lived at number eighty-seven. She gave Zu Zu a jar of Pretty Peach crème perfume for Christmas. She used to throw various kitchen utensils, books, slippers, tins of talc, anything near to hand, it seemed, from upstairs windows.

Some of the neighbours who had been hit by flying objects complained to the council and petitioned unsuccessfully for a polite warning to be placed on a lamp post for passing pedestrians. Usually posh Lucinda Hancock dropped her Hs and threatened them all with a broken nose, shouting, 'Not bloody well likely.' Mrs Hancock was having none of it. She went on to tell anyone who would listen that she did what she had to do.

'It's my dead husband, you see,' Mrs Hancock told Zu Zu's mum one day. 'You remember Archie, don't you? Well, he's a ghost now. He comes back for me every other night, crafty bastard, stands over there by the lamp post winking at me, telling me he's tired of waiting. He's haunting me, moving things around the house. I'm going to see if Vicar Wickham can help me. It's not right.' Mrs Hancock started sniffling, put her shopping bags down and pulled a paper hanky from her pocket.

'Perhaps he just misses you, love. Must be lonely on the other side,' Zu Zu's mum said.

'Misses me? He bloody well wants me dead! Well, he can clear off and go back to wherever it is he's come from and leave me in peace. There's life in these old bones yet.'

Zu Zu's mum nodded. 'Of course, dear. It can't be easy for you.' Smiling weakly, Lucinda Hancock lifted up her bags of shopping and walked home to number eighty-seven.

The next day, after delivering a few copies of the *Radio Times*, the *Daily Express* and *The People's Friend*, Zu Zu checked the assortment of belongings on the ground by the lamp post at number eighty-seven. She found an unopened packet of garibaldi biscuits and a hardback Oxford English Dictionary. Grinning, she carefully picked them up and placed them on Mrs Hancock's doormat beside a pair of empty milk bottles.

The Jehovah's Witness Kingdom Hall was on the opposite corner. Its white noticeboard promised that beyond those walls was Heaven, but Zu Zu suspected this wasn't true because no one was queuing – or perhaps Heaven was full or not open today. By the time she arrived at number nineteen, she knew she was halfway through her paper round. She could hear raised voices coming from inside the house. Men's voices, raw and ragged. Quietly, Zu Zu crouched down and did what she was always told not to; she looked through the letterbox.

Two men were struggling in the narrow hallway, their bodies a dark, moving tangle.

One man staggered, his back to the door, a knife held in his hand. He ran forward and stabbed the other man again and again. The sound was the same as the one she made when cutting deep into soft fruit.

The other man fell forward and made a heavy, final sound as his body hit the floor. Zu Zu felt a warm trickle run down her legs, forming a puddle around her black Mary Jane shoes. Quickly she let go of the letterbox flap – but not before seeing the murderer turn at the sound of the noise. Her dad stared back at her. Zu Zu screamed and ran down the path, her pigtails flying. She dropped her pile of printed words, sending newspapers and magazines sprawling across the pavement. When she got home, she rushed up the staircase to the bathroom. 'Where's the fire?' her mum called up the stairs, then shook her head and returned to her knitting.

Zu Zu didn't talk for a whole year. During that time, she was assessed by an educational psychologist, a speech therapist, a clinical psychologist, a paediatrician and a child psychiatrist, who all found her to be 'functioning within the normal range', but she was still unable to speak. The professionals agreed that she had been traumatised, but couldn't say how. Her dad trod on eggshells. The big, sulky cloud loomed over her and clapped his hands cheerily as if trying to rally a losing Spurs side at half-time.

Zu Zu, who had only ever killed bluebottles and earwigs, couldn't look at him, and her red and black drawings of darkened hallways held meaning only for herself and her dad. She believed the whites of his eyes were missing and dodged his smile. Like a room cut off from sunlight, she became shuttered.

Every birthday, her dad bought her increasingly expensive presents, while her mum continued to talk to her loudly and slowly as if she was hard of hearing, cutting up her words and sentences like she cut up Zu Zu's sausages.

H described Zu Zu's childhood as dysregulating and problematic. He said her home was a home of secrets, turned backs and criminality and her trauma had gone untreated. The dead man, Harry Swan, was a well-known Tottenham villain. Police reports confirmed that he had owed large sums of money to various mob bosses. It was described as a revenge killing. Someone had grassed him up. Must have done. It was local opinion that Harry Swan had got what was coming to him. Zu Zu never told, and no one was ever arrested for the crime.

When she met Kenny the shutters were raised. He was like a freshly minted sixpence, shiny and new. He mesmerised Zu Zu with his dreams.

'Babe, I'm gonna make it big and then I'll buy us a French chateau. We'll have orchards, a pig farm, land you can't see the end of. Felix, my mate, says he knows a man who knows a lot about pigs. Breeding. And then there's wine. You know I've got green fingers, I can grow anything. We can just go, pack up and go. My luck's turning. I can feel it, babe. Like something big's on its way. You wait and see, Zu Zu, just wait and see. With the money I make from that job Leroy told me about and with a bit of luck on the horses, we'll be halfway there. You'll see.'

Kenny was bony and wiry like a coat hanger, but a man of excesses. He had big ideas, big dreams and he swore blind that everything was bigger, brighter than it was. He said that he saw rats as big as cats, tits as big as juggernauts, rubbed shoulders with people so rich they could buy Buckingham

Palace twice over. The more drink Kenny had, the looser his lips became. Zu Zu always knew what was coming, the next big idea, the next get-rich-quick scheme. His narrow shoulders seemed resistant to growth, lagging behind a large head full of thought and imagination.

'He's black,' her mum said, as if pouring away spoilt milk.

'Tell me something I don't know.'

'It won't go down well with your dad.'

'I don't care what Dad thinks or doesn't think.'

'And he's from the Farm. Dear Lord, the place is overrun with criminals.'

Zu Zu stared at her mum. 'Are you being serious? You don't know anything about Kenny or the Farm. You wouldn't know decent if it came and hit you in the face.'

Her mum lunged forward as if to strike, but Zu Zu stepped back and said, 'Don't you dare. You lay a finger on me, Mother, and I swear to God, I'll knock you down where you stand.'

Lowering her arm, her mum shifted her attention to the dirty dishes in the kitchen sink; she didn't say another word. Zu Zu's parents were friendly with Mr and Mrs Oluwole and they were black, but Mr Oluwole drove a new jag and Mrs Oluwole worked in Barclays bank.

When Zu Zu brought Kenny home to meet her parents, her dad left the house before they arrived. He told her mum to tell her that he had to see a man about something. After Kenny left, her mum said, 'His colour is something. I mean, he's proper dark. You know, like black – not even brown-black, but real dark black.'

'Yeah, he's beautiful.'

'You need to think of the children you would have with him.'

'Yes, they'd be beautiful, too.'

'And I don't like his eyes, not one bit – shifty.'

'Glass houses,' Zu Zu said.

When Zu Zu and Kenny got married at Wood Green Civic Centre, her parents didn't attend the ceremony but old schoolfriends like Veronica Walton and Daphne Patterson came and showered Kenny and Zu Zu in lemon and white horseshoe confetti that stuck to the ground when the light drizzle turned to dense sheets of rain. Money was lean but they moved away from Tottenham and into a studio flat in Peckham where they found delights in a second-hand single bed.

On the November night when Kenny was killed, he left Zu Zu, Johnny and Frankie behind and took his dreams with him. Zu Zu was flooded all over again and, like a paper boat, she folded and sank. She lost her voice, her strength, her home, her children. It took time to resurface. H said she'd done extremely well, considering.

Zu Zu could drive round the corner right now and park outside the Social Services head office. She could ask, could demand her children's return and wait. And then place her faultless children in the passenger seats. Seatbelt them safely inside. They would sit quietly like good children, small hands neatly folded in their laps. Straight, pearly-white teeth. Sunday best children; the boy with the summer smile and the girl with spongy candyfloss hair. And Zu Zu would drive and drive and drive. She would never stop, because destinations are fixed points that need explanations.

Zu Zu heads home through the rush-hour traffic and back to Willan Road, Broadwater Farm. She smiles at skateboarding Ricky and Kevin as she drives by, and in return they give her little waves and mischievous grins. Later that night, struggling to sleep, she wanders into her small back garden.

Old plastic flowerpots line a low stone wall that separates the small decked patio from the lawn. In the black earth of flower beds and flowerpots are green shoots waiting for spring.

Zu Zu squats on a patch of slightly damp lawn and lets out a heavy sigh. Flopping back onto the grass, she pulls her dressing gown tightly around her and stares up at the stars. There are trillions, zillions of them. Worlds of certain light. She imagines the parallel universes she could occupy, the different lives she might lead. In at least one universe, Zu Zu lives with Kenny and her children. She is an attentive and devoted mother, wiping runny noses, reading bedtime stories, kissing bruised knees and loving her children to the moon and back, and back again.

A fleck of flickering golden light skirts across the night sky, growing brigher. Twirling, ducking, diving. Quickly, she sits up and rubs her eyes. It's been a long day, and an even longer life. She can't be sure, but she thinks she spots a figure with wings, flying nearer and nearer. She's been drinking Horlicks, not cider, and still she suspects she's seeing things that aren't there. She stands up, loosens her dressing gown, tosses her head back and shouts up at the sky, 'Hey, hey, take me with you. Take me.' Splaying her arms, she cries out, 'It's me, Zu Zu. Zu Zu. Take me with you.' The golden light draws closer. This isn't a gin devil, ancient curse or rumble from the past but something different. She squints – she has always been short-sighted and isn't sure what it is she sees now. Reaching up, the milky-white moon held in a hand, Zu Zu wonders how it is that although she touches the skies with her fingertips, her feet remain firmly planted on the Farm's solid ground. A new smile lights her face; it's another mystery, she muses, another mystery. To herself she whispers, 'I am alive to the world and the world is alive to me.'

XIV

Ricky's Story

Above our heads is a shepherd's delight or guava jelly sky, depending on who's looking up.

'You won't believe it, but the other day I saw a dog with two legs humping another dog,' says Kev, leaning against a climbing frame. Kev's blazer hangs off his shoulders and his black trousers balloon around his bandy legs. Everyone knows bandy guys make the best footballers. I used to sleep with pillows between my legs to make mine bandy, but it didn't work and I'm always stuck in goal.

Kev's spouting rubbish again. There's no such thing as a two-legged dog. How could it stand up, let alone do anything else?

The only weird thing I know about for sure is old Bill Birmingham streaking round the Farm singing 'I Shot the Sheriff'. Bill does this most Christmases and it's not even that weird anymore, it's kind of a Farm tradition.

'Where d'ya see a two-legged dog having sex?' I ask, rubbing my annoyingly hairless chin before doing a kickflip on my skateboard.

'Instagram.' Kev lowers his voice. 'But between you and me, the weirdest thing I ever saw was in Edmonton.'

I know I'm about to hear more from Kev about his conspiracy theories. He's always doing online 'research' into aliens and otherworldly stuff. He's got a collection of *Ripley's Believe It or Not* books dating back to 1976.

'Please not that illuminati stuff again,' I sigh.

'Look, Ricky, I know what I know and you don't know what you don't know. I'm woke and I've seen stuff, you get me?'

'Like?'

'That black Cadillac I told you about. The driver's got demon-red eyes – I actually saw him. Pasty white face and a black hat. He drives round Tottenham and Edmonton Green at night, nicking kids and stuffing them in his boot.'

'Red eyes and stealing kids?'

'Yeah, red eyes and stealing kids.'

I take a deep gulp from a can of Lilt.

'Remember when Marlon Jones went missing?' Kev says. 'He wasn't right when he came back – he's still a bit spaced. I reckon the bloke with the red eyes took him. Edmonton is seriously spooky. Mix up the letters and Edmonton is Demonton. Demon Town. Join the dots, fam.'

Kev drones on. 'These demons won't win, of course, because there are angels working for the other side. You see, there's a war going on between the forces of good and evil, and good always triumphs in the end.' He gives me a big soppy grin, showing his wide gums and neat teeth.

Being a brilliant striker and a sick dancer means Kev's got special ranking at our school. He's been signed up for Spurs under-eighteens and is even treated with a special kind of reverence by some of the teachers. Mr Daley always lets Kev off if he hasn't done his English Lit homework, says he understands the pressures of professional football. Kev isn't the only one with knowledge or secrets, but I'm not saying a word about the strangest thing I've seen. This is my secret and I hold it tightly like a talisman in my pocket. Every time I think about it, bolts of excitement race through my body, because it means anything's possible and everything can change. No more mucking out on the Farm.

I check my phone. There's a text from Mum asking me where I am and why I'm late. 'I've got to boot, bro. Safe.'

We don't play on the climbing frame or swinging tyres anymore; we're black, sixteen and have lived on Broadwater Farm all our lives. I live on Willan Road and Kev lives on the tenth floor of Kenley, with clear views of Ally Pally and fireworks on New Year's Eve.

Whenever I walk through the Farm, the words 'my home' touch doors, walls, windows, fences, murals, playgrounds, towers, small squares of green grass and dark, grey walkways. This is my village, my manor, my yard, and it's tough but pretty cool. In the summer the drains reek. We've been told it's because of the Moselle River in Lordship Recreation Ground becoming polluted with liquid waste and sewage. The council posted notices through every door saying they were sorting out the misconnected pipes upstream, but we reckon the sewage runs down from posh Muswell Hill and the council can't find the exact houses to blame. Whatever the reason, every year from June to August we get crapped on and suffer the big stink. And after Grenfell, the council said eleven of our towers are at risk of disaster if ever there's a fire; the word is that Tangmere and Northolt will have to be demolished and people rehoused, including my mum's boyfriend Popeye.

I know all my neighbours, like Brother Marcus who leads the Broadwater Farm Gospel Singers, beer-belly Amos who walks around with a trailing dog lead, but there's no dog since Prince got run over, Pastor Luke who preaches in the church on the Farm every Sunday, and Latoya Mitchell, the pengest girl in school, tailed by boys with not the remotest chance of ever getting close. This Farm, these people, these blocks, these roads are my home. It's not Toyland, you've got to keep your eyes open, but you've got to use street-smarts wherever you are, it's just the way it is, the way we live now.

There's a poster on the Neighbourhood Office door calling for residents to take part in a photo opportunity as part of a community project.

There are at least four thousand people living here – that would be an amazing photo. The poster says there are people from at least forty countries living on the Farm and I've been trying to list what those countries could be. Sometimes it feels like we've got the whole world here on our Farm.

In pastel colours, Marley, Ghandi and Lennon look down from the Peace Mural. Martin Luther King Jr surveys them from a mountaintop. Bob's the only one laughing; Gandhi and Lennon look serious – might be something to do with their glasses. I can see the mural from my bedroom window. I like the figures in the foreground, dancing to the music coming from a big sound system.

Voices and laughter come from a group standing near the bus stop. Tiny bops towards me, a glide in his stride. A blue baseball cap shadows his lean face and a toothpick works his mouth. Tiny's real name is Sean Cherry. He's wide like a wall and stands over six feet tall. Like a tree, he blocks out the late afternoon sun. He's older than me but we both went to Woodlands primary school.

'Yo, Icky Ricky.'

My throat closes in a fog of weed smoke. Tiny and his crew pick up odd jobs when they can. Labouring and building-site work some of the time, but mainly other stuff.

'How's your old man?' Tiny asks.

'Okay.' I swallow hard.

'Still living south of the drink?'

'Yep.'

'With the same woman? The one he left your mum for?'

'Yeah.'

'I remember when your dad drove round last summer. Brand new Audi. Old skool funk coming out the windows. When he went into your house to pick you up, we all walked over to get a better look of his car. We weren't gonna do anything, but his new missus quickly wound up the windows, pulled at each door. I mean, she locked those doors so damn tight, like she didn't even want air to get in, and then she starts beeping the horn. Man, did we laugh.'

Our heads turn as a car floats by, pumping loud drill music rhythms.

'Your dad is cool though, blud. That Sports Day when he was in the three-legged race with Mr Jackson and they fell over in the mud?' Tiny laughs and I remember Dad's mud-caked face. 'I'll never forget that day. Those were the good days back then – but things change.' He takes a long drag from his spliff.

'And what about Justine Redd?' he asks.

Justine Redd. How can I ever forget Justine Redd? My first and last girlfriend. Soft, liquid mocha-brown eyes and a cheeky gap between two front teeth. The Woodland Trail. The taste of hot salty chips on my tongue.

He stares. 'Did you give her one?'

'Course.'

I didn't even get to second base. Justine never called or texted back.

'We used to call her Ever-Ready.' Tiny shrugs. 'Her family got a transfer. She's living in Milton Keynes now. Doing a Business Studies course. We've been to the Neighbourhood Office and put our names down for a transfer, too. My family could be next to move out. Don't you want to move?'

'Go where?'

Tiny shrugs. 'Dunno. Anywhere.'

I shake my head. Tiny's very, very smart, he keeps up with everything. Quicksilver with words, he always knows what's happening on the Farm.

'Your mum should do it,' he says. 'That's how you move up the food chain.'

'The Farm's okay.'

'It's poisoned and polluted, man.'

'Some people are doing all right.'

'Yeah, only the ones who move out. Try putting Broadwater Farm on a job application form. I've been to the Job Centre and the Opportunities Office – load of bullshit. They don't offer you anything.'

'The Farm's my home.'

'More like fucking prison. You can't see the bars, Ricky boy, but you will.'

Tiny has three baby mothers on the Farm. He looks after his kids, takes them to the park and the movies. The women used to spit gravel at one another when they first found out Tiny worked them to his timetable – they had a punch-up outside the Children's Centre. But now they're best friends, like sisters. I guess hate can burn itself out.

His younger brother Clay goes to the special school. I've seen Tiny pushing Clay's wheelchair, taking him to watch Spurs at White Hart Lane. With quiet dedication he taught Clay to clap with his bent, twisted fingers. Here on the street though, Tiny acts as hard as the ground he walks on. Smiling, he tugs a wallet from his pocket, flashing a fat wad of notes.

'There's plenty more where this came from, Ricky. Easy money if you're up to doing another run. We'll bring the gear and you do the drop. No county lines, we keep it local. Hampstead, Highgate, Muswell Hill, usual places, usual stuff.'

Each word is broken down into separate syllables as if he can multiply their meaning and slow time. I know the usual stuff. E. Skunk. Spice. Weed. Crack. Coke.

After my last run, I threw up, my stomach buckling until it was empty. I decided that was it, I was never going to do another run. It just wasn't worth it. The fear, the cost if I got caught, the danger that had stopped being exciting and the hurt it would cause Mum. Although Tiny is a big voice in the Broadwater crew and the Young Warriors gang, he has enemies and has to watch his back. Last year, his best friend and sidekick Fitzroy was stabbed; he died on the way to the hospital. There are ongoing wars between different gangs and I want no part of it, never did.

'Go on, surprise me,' Tiny whispers, ash breath in my face. 'Say yes.'

My stammer's about to surface, tripping up my tongue, but I say nothing.

He chuckles. 'Nah, didn't think so.'

I definitely need new trainers. Looking down at my feet I imagine them inside a brand-new pair of Yeezys.

'Things will change now we've got the new Spurs stadium. There'll be new jobs and the area will go up, you'll see,' I say, trying to spread my hope.

'Oh, Icky Ricky, you still don't get it, do you? The stadium is just another Trojan horse. It ain't the big fix people think it is. The stadium regeneration in Rio had people marching in the streets. They fixed the stadium but they didn't fix the favelas – the people got fuck all. Big money don't trickle down. And before you mention the plans to fix up the Farm, let me tell you, all that regeneration talk is just about bulldozing the place and shipping us all out to God knows where. That's why your mum should jump before she's pushed.'

'Or we can stay, fight back and make things better. Anyway, I heard that Haringey council has ended its deal with the developers.'

Tiny frowns. 'Really? I'm not sure about that – there are still plans to knock down Tangmere and Northolt.'

'Yeah, so I heard.'

'And we still don't know what's going to be built in their place. Look, however you dress it up, Ricky, so-called regeneration is just a pretty word for social cleansing.'

'Well, I like being positive.'

'Positive? Just how many people do you think will be able to afford to come back and live here once they've demolished those blocks and the Farm and built fancy new homes? Certainly not people like you and me.'

There's been a lot of talk on the estate, meetings in the community centre and marches on Tottenham High Road.

We even had a discussion about regeneration in our general studies class at school. I just want what's best for the Farm, and I know I've got a lot more to learn and understand. Stubbing out the last bit of spliff, Tiny brings himself up to his full height.

'Well, if you change your mind about doing a bit of work and earning some cash, you know where to find me.'

I remember when Tiny, the school bully, used to chase me round the school playground calling me Pissy Pants. He would break it down into three long syllables: piss-ee-pants.

'Oh, and tell your dad he owes me a game of pool,' Tiny says before he walks away.

As I run home, my rucksack feels like a hump on my back. I dodge the heavy downpour that licks the Farm gravestone-grey, but with or without the rain I know the Farm's every sound. It has a heartbeat, a calling, a waiting, and I want to be part of the turnaround, the better times that I know are coming. With my secret, suddenly nothing's impossible.

The television's on, it's always on, filling the flat with people, while Mum sits alone on the sofa. She's curled up on a heart-shaped cushion, her small afro flattened on one side where she's been resting her head.

'All right, love?' she asks, sitting up and wiping her mouth.

'Yeah. Fancy a hot chocolate, Mum?' I throw my book bag and skateboard in the small space under the stairs.

'That would be nice.'

She leans forward and watches me fill the kettle with water. 'I saw you talking with Sean Cherry or whatever stupid name he calls himself.'

'Tiny.'

'Yeah, like I said, whatever stupid name he calls himself.

He's no good, Ricky. I don't want you to have anything to do with him. I went to school with his mum, Keisha. She's a nasty piece of work. They're trouble, that family, all of them. They've always got the Old Bill sniffing around. Most people on the Farm are hard-working, decent, but not them – they're the exception.'

'I can take care of myself, Mum.'

'I hope so. He's been hanging out with Enzo Kaya and Dit Ahmeti – everyone knows those two are seriously bad news. Just promise me you'll stay away from them.'

'Mum, I don't have anything to do with Dit or Enzo, but I've known Tiny since I was a kid – he's not all bad,' I say, thinking about Tiny with his brother.

'I reckon when it comes to life and people, I know a lot more than you do. We might not start out all bad or all good, but make life hard enough and even the best people can go wrong.'

There she goes, treating me like the weedy kid I used to be in primary school. Mum can't accept that I'm growing up – she wants to keep me tied to her, but I'm not her little boy anymore and I know more than she realises. We see different things when we look out of the kitchen window. I imagine what I can't see, an exciting future that could be there, but I know Mum sees what she knows. I've got dreams and ambitions she's never even asked me about. Dad says getting qualifications is my way up and out, but Tiny and his posse wait for me to fall, wait for me to join them.

Some of my mates are always telling me how my dice are loaded, how I can't go far, even though I'm straight-As Ricky Thompson. Geek in glasses, too bright to be black.

Sometimes I want to smash everything into the smallest of pieces, but I imagine that if my anger erupts somehow it will sink the Farm and reduce the village I love to nothing but rubble, so I push my anger down and keep it hidden under books, dreams and good grades. No one asks what I want. I want to date Maya Jama, rap with Stormzy or Skepta and be Britain's first black Prime Minister. Sometimes I'm squeezed until I'm about to burst, and when that happens I blast Stormzy, making the walls and floors throb until Mum calls out, 'Ricky Thompson, turn that noise down, I can't hear myself think.'

Mum's left sausage rolls on a plate and a big plate of vegetables and macaroni cheese in the microwave. She works at Greggs and always brings food home. Heaping two teaspoons of powdered hot chocolate into a mug along with sugar and milk, I stir the mixture into a smooth, creamy paste. I've done this a hundred times.

Dad left five years ago. There had been brick-wall silences and daily rows. On the day he left, he took me into the hallway and said, 'You need to know none of this is your fault, son.' He looked over my shoulder at the open door to the living room where Mum sat watching television with the sound suddenly turned down. Under his arms he gripped vinyl discs storing the sounds of John Coltrane, Charlie Parker and Miles Davis as if he carried bars of gold. He handed me his front-door keys, and I waited for him to look back and wave or smile or do whatever it is parents do if they leave, but he didn't.

Mum didn't say much and for months I never heard or saw her cry. She gave me shopping lists and sent me on expeditions to Tesco. Neighbours asked, 'How's your mum? Is she okay?' and I nodded, but I wasn't sure. When I asked her, Mum said, 'Sometimes life is like swallowing the sea, and when it really hurts somehow you have to learn to breathe underwater.' I didn't understand what she meant and the cloudy look in her eyes told me not to ask her any more about how she was feeling. It was only when she cut her middle finger opening a can of runner beans that things changed. I heard her yelp and, running downstairs, I saw her blood spouting like a fountain.

We took a mini-cab to A&E at North Middlesex Hospital and sat in a waiting room full of bloodied and broken people. Mum turned to me and said, 'Get me a cup of tea, love,' but when I came back empty-handed and told her the drinks machine wasn't working, fat tears started streaming down her face.

'Just once...' she said. 'If something could work out just once – but it never does. I didn't know I'd been asking for the moon all this bloody time.'

Mum cried hard. She squeezed out every bit of sea, and I knew she was getting better.

Three years later and for the first time since Dad left, Mum and Dad went to parents' evening together, sat next to each other and congratulated me on my grades.

Mum said, 'He's still your dad, no matter what I think of him.'

Dad's new wife, India (he calls her Indie), is thinner and younger than Mum and serves up cold snacks she doesn't eat. Most of the time the two of them live on green smoothies made with spirulina and chia seeds. All the drinks look like Halloween witches' brews and taste like stewed cabbage. India is straight lines whereas mum is cuddly curves. She often claps her hands and chirps, 'Happy, happy, happy,' reminding me of those hyper TV presenters on kids' programmes.

India works as a life coach and has a shiny, waxy face that always looks surprised. Around the walls of their Brixton house hang paintings with scenes of beaches and mountains with captions like 'No such thing as failure, just feedback', and 'A journey of a thousand miles starts with a single step'.

Dad laughs more now and plays practical jokes, like the time he handed us dessert dishes stacked with vegan apple crumble, but he had swapped soya cream for shaving foam. India and I nearly choked. I can't remember him ever playing practical jokes at home or laughing much.

'Still pulling those grades, Ricky? Keep at it, son. The jobless figure for black guys is fifty per cent. It's tough out there, yunno, but you've got to fight the system and keep working hard. Don't ever forget you've got choices – you don't have to fall in with the Sean Cherrys of the world, you're better than that. Guys like him are losers, ain't going anywhere. But look at Patrick Fuller, he's at medical school now. That could be you, Ricky, God knows all your teachers say you're smart enough.' Push. Push. Push. Dad's push and Mum's pull are just part of my family scenery. Life is full of waves and tides but I just about know how to surf.

Dad doesn't talk with me; he preaches and coaches like he's preparing me for life in a boxing ring. Each time he speaks, he piles pressure on my shoulders.

With a Brillo pad I scrub a greasy saucepan, and my cuffs are damp when I walk into the living room. Taking her mug, Mum says, 'Mick and L are fighting again.' She talks about soap characters as if they're family. I tell Mum that I bumped into Cupcake earlier.

Cupcake is a family friend who has taken me and Mum under her wing ever since Great-Grandma Willa died. She lives on Stapleford, and a month ago she lost her job at Curry's.

'How is she?'

'Yes, she's doing okay, said she's got a new job at Pearsons in Enfield.'

Mum nods, her eyes not shifting from the screen. 'That's good. She told me she had an interview.'

Mum only talks when adverts are on. Once she changes channels and the screen shows *EastEnders*, she's gone.

In the kitchen I make my dinner: a macaroni cheese, sausage roll, peanut butter, vegetables (to keep Mum happy) and ketchup sandwich and a triple-chocolate muffin dunked in a long glass of milk.

Sucking on my secret, I think about Popeye, Mum's boyfriend. Popeye lives on Northolt block and is the first person people go to when they have a burst pipe or a cat gets stuck up a tree. On Saturdays he mentors kids in the community centre. I like having him around, but it felt strange the first time I caught Mum and Popeye kissing. I saw Mum being held like a bunch of flowers by a man who wasn't my dad. Once I overheard Mum and Cupcake talking. Cupcake said, 'Forget about Mr Perfect, you've got Mr More-Than-Good-Enough. Denzel Washington isn't coming and neither is Idris Elba but Popeye's here. This is your "At Last", so just you let your love-light shine and go with the flow.' Mum has always had crushes on Denzel Washington and Idris Elba, but she let Popeye into our lives and seems happier than she has been in a long time.

Mum and I met Popeye at a community meeting after the riots in 2011 when I was in Year Three. On the night of the riots, we stayed inside and listened to the background music of police and fire-engine sirens. Mum told me it was like the bad old days of 1985. She was just seven when those riots happened; she remembers the terror, rage and fear, and the deaths of two people.

In assembly that Monday morning, our headteacher Mrs Barrymore, clearing her throat, spoke about the need for calm. When the police inspector beside her stood to speak, Clinton Perry in Year Six kissed his teeth loudly and the policeman froze.

Clinton was given a week's suspension. Like a silent army, all the boys walked around with hunched shoulders as if we were getting ready for a fight. The enemy was anyone who wasn't us and didn't know or believe what we knew.

Reporters and journalists waved microphones at our neighbours, asking for opinions and eyewitness accounts but Mum walked past, head up, and offered nothing.

'We don't want any trouble,' she said to them. 'I've got nothing to say.'

One afternoon in August, I came home from football practice and found Mum smoking. I couldn't remember her smoking since I'd been at school.

'What's up?'

She gave a half-smile. 'Marva Dixon called me a coward. She said I should speak up, tell the reporters how hard our lives are, what help we need. She said I wasn't helping and that I should make my voice heard, tell them what I know, tell the truth. Whatever that is.'

'Just ignore her,' I said, giving Mum the same advice she always gave me.

Mum stubbed out the cigarette. 'Marva said if I'm not part of the solution, I'm part of the problem. I told her straight, I didn't want to speak to anyone. I remember what happened to my oldest brother, your uncle, when we did just that. Our family paid the price. Your uncle Jimmy just disappeared, never to be seen or heard of again. A note was posted through our front door. A little piece of white paper with one four-letter word: shhh. The Old Bill said they would do what they could, and now Jimmy's just registered as missing... Missing must be the most hollowed-out word in the English language.'

She looked through the kitchen window which faces the small green outside.

'Now it's about our family, our safety and survival – and because of that, what I know stays in here,' and she tapped the side of her head with her brown fingers. 'I'm not taking any risks and I'm not talking to any reporters, newspaper people or anyone. I'm keeping my mouth shut.'

Later that night, I heard Mum crying. I've asked her about things that happened but she waves away my questions, saying, 'Ricky, you don't need to know about this stuff.' But I want to know; I get tired of her shutting me out.

A lot of people got sent down in 2011. Looting and possession of stolen goods. Kev's older brother Tyson got banged up for stealing an electric guitar and Fiona Lewis was caught with a television. Rihanna Hutchins got six months for stealing a case of bottled mineral water. But not everyone got caught. The Petrol brothers, Teapot and Kaz, had a visit from the feds. They kept quiet, said they knew nothing. Teapot and Kaz were the lucky ones. I remember wet bedsheets and the cold sweat of nightmares in which I was chased through a winding labyrinth of dead-end Tottenham backstreets by white-faced, dark-suited bogeymen.

'It'll all blow over soon enough,' Dad said. 'We've just got to keep our heads down.' He remembers 1985 but tells me it's best to forget. 'Your grandad used to say "Don't waste white powder on a black bird." Forward facing, Ricky, forward facing.'

At the community meeting, when most people spoke, Popeye was silent. He was new to the Farm. His bald head was a shiny brown four-point snooker ball and his raven-black eyes whizzed left and right. I noticed the telephone scar that stretched from Popeye's mouth to his ear, the sure sign of a snitch.

'He must have grassed up the wrong person, got his hands dirty,' Kev whispered. 'That's why he's zipping it.' He figured Popeye was Old Bill or a spy; either way, a telephone scar meant trouble.

Weeks after the meeting, Popeye held a party and most of Northolt block turned up. He said it was his way of helping things get back to normal. The party grew and spilled outside. Armchairs and tables were carried onto Lordship Recreation Ground, and people from the Farm partied on the grass and by the Shell Theatre. Everyone ate jerk chicken and bammy, drank their bellies full of Guinness punch and did the Electric Slide. Old black and white men took their seats on a corner of the green, looking like squares on a chessboard. They roared and slammed dominoes late into the night. This was when the Farm was best, when the concrete and the past didn't matter, when we were just people, doing what people do. The Farm is an island – it changes shape with the tides and weather, but always bounces back.

Just before ten o'clock, Mum yawns and says, 'Right, I'm off to bed.' With a big sigh, she lifts herself up from the sofa. 'Don't stay up late, you've got school tomorrow, and be a love and bolt the front door before you come up.'

Turning off the television, I remember the weirdest thing I've ever seen and shivers of excitement shockwave down from my head to my toes. My secret. It was two days ago when I first saw it. Maybe I'll see it again tonight. I head up to my den, where the sign on the door reads 'Ricky's Den – Keep Out', and most of the time Mum does.

Jumpers and jeans lie tangled on the floor, and Marvel and DC comics borrowed from Kev's collection poke out from under my bed. In lurid, swirling colours the *Fantastic Four*, *Judge Dredd*, *Wolverine*, *Deadpool*, *Doctor Thirteen*, *Avengers Universe* and the *Phantom Stranger* stare up at me.

Walking over to my bedroom window, I pull back the curtains to see a blue-black sky stapled with stars. I've got a clear view of Northolt block. Streetlights cover the side of the building in a soft, smoky haze. Popeye's flat has two windows on this side, and further along balcony doors open onto a small patio where he keeps his telescope. When Mum and I first visited Popeye's flat on the seventeenth floor of Northolt, he showed us the telescope, a Galaxy AstroMaster 130EQ with motor drive. He said that the latest telescopes were so advanced you could see thirty-five million galaxies, one every twenty minutes. Mum shivered and said, 'It's too nippy for me, guys. I'm going back inside.' She smiled and closed the balcony doors behind her.

'The moon's up,' Popeye said, 'take a look.' He's an engineer with BT, but he says this is his hobby, his passion.

Pointing upwards, he said, 'There's Orion's Belt... and that's the North Star.'

He talked about light pollution, humidity, transparency and atmosphere all affecting what we can see, but he said it was a perfect night for viewing.

'Turbulence is a mystery,' Popeye said, sticking his hands in his pockets. 'It creates problems seeing but it also makes the stars twinkle. There's a flip side to most things.'

I had problems focusing at first. Popeye said not to look at the stars but to look around them, to use what he called my averted vision. When the stars looked back I thought I could touch them, thought I could feel the lumps and bumps of the moon's acne-cratered face. Popeye swerved the telescope around and told me to take another look.

'That's Sirius,' he said, 'the brightest star system in the night sky. One of Earth's closest neighbours and twice as big as the sun.'

Popeye asked me different questions: 'What can you see? How faint is it? How bright? What colour?' The image was unsteady on my eye, but I could see Sirius, all shades of blue and yellow, a quivering ball of light vibrating like it was about to shatter.

'There are secrets out there, Ricky, dimensions and realities outside the limits of space and time. Life isn't just what is but also what could be.'

I was a squillion miles from Broadwater Farm. When I had enough money I would buy a telescope so I could leave the Farm, Tottenham, Haringey, North London, England, the United Kingdom, Europe, the Northern Hemisphere, the world, whenever I wanted.

Popeye chatted away while I looked on. 'Caribbean legend says that's where we black people come from. Sirius.'

'You sound like Kev – he's always coming out with stuff like that.'

'Perhaps your mate Kev's got more smarts than you think.'

Popeye swivelled the telescope. 'And that's where Heaven is, just there, behind Orion's belt. About three billion light years away.'

He said this in a matter-of-fact way, like he was reading from a shopping list. I made out a speckled, milky blue region that looked like the inside of a marble. Next he'd be saying the Farm was built on ley lines or the site of King Arthur's Camelot. I wondered if Popeye was some kind of magician or wizard. The Wizard of Broadwater Farm. He seemed more at home looking up at the night sky than he was down here, feet on the ground.

When we went back into the living room Mum was dancing to 'Toast' by Koffee, winding her waist like she does each year at the Notting Hill Carnival. Her eyeliner had run and muddy smudges circled her eyes. She wore the leopard-print dress she normally saved for Christmas. It was a bit tight under the arms and earlier she'd asked if she could get away with it; I nodded but didn't know what to say. When Mum asks questions, a lot of the time I haven't got answers.

'All good, Ricky?' she asked.

'Yeah, all good, Mum.' She gave Popeye a red lip-glossy smile and mouthed, 'Thank you.'

The time on my phone is now 3.10am. I'm just about to move away from the window and go to bed when I see the balcony doors slowly open and Popeye step onto his small patio. Then the weirdest thing happens. Again. Carefully, Popeye climbs up onto the balcony and balances on the edge, his arms outstretched.

He lifts his face up to the sky and suddenly two large, white, feathery wings sprout from his body. Popeye fans his wings and rises up into the night. Flying above the rooftops, scaffolding, dumped mattresses and concrete towers, he looks like he's dancing. As his body twirls, loops, dips and dives,

Popeye radiates a glowing, golden light. I wonder if anyone else is watching, but the Farm is silent and still. No streaking Bill Birmingham tonight.

Gradually, Popeye flutters down and lands on the patio, where he bends and holds his knees like he's getting his breath back. Suddenly he freezes and steps forward, looking straight in my direction. I duck and crouch below the window frame. Idiot. What if he's seen me? I should have been more careful. Peeping from behind the curtains, I watch Popeye close the balcony doors.

I'm not imagining it. Popeye can actually fly. This thought bounces round my head like a ping-pong ball. He has to be an angel, one of the good guys. My mind spins. Popeye's not a spy or Old Bill. Not sure about the telephone scar – perhaps he's a recent convert, a good guy who used to be bad or a fallen angel who broke ranks, teamed up with God and pissed off Satan. Perhaps he's come to save the Farm or save the planet. Anything is possible. And obviously it's very complicated.

A few months ago, at home with the flu and lying on the sofa, I watched daytime TV. A guest on *Good Morning Britain* said she'd been living with angels all her life, but the angels she described were all white, nine feet tall with blonde hair and blue eyes. Popeye is about five foot nine and black. I picked up my laptop and typed in 'angels'. I discovered there are all sorts of angels. Ethnicity and height don't come into it. Angels are diverse.

Someone online reckons they are given jobs helping, protecting; they spend their days, invisibly most of the time, in prisons and hospitals, beside bridges and railway tracks, anywhere they can comfort and guide. Some have wings, others don't; one angel was described as having as many as 140 pairs of wings. Maybe Popeye is a guardian angel sent here to make everything okay. Thinking this makes my heart swell. Perhaps he'll help turn the Farm around, fix all the things that are broken, clean up the Moselle River, sort out the drains and dissolve the prison bars Tiny says I can't see. Thinking back to the *Good Morning Britain* woman, I decide she was an ignorant saddo.

Late for school the next day, I earn a detention with my form tutor. Miss Moss looks exactly how my big sister would have looked if I had one. She has dark walnut-coloured skin, wears designer glasses that are too big for her small, elfin face and her hair is styled in tight china bumps that line her head in rows. Letting me out from detention ten minutes early, she gives me one of her over-the-glasses stern-warning looks. 'Next time there'll be detention *and* lines, Ricky.' I hunt for Kev but can't find him; he's probably training in the community centre's sports hall for the Middlesex Schools cup final.

When I get home I hear voices coming from the kitchen. Mum's dipping a teabag in a mug and Popeye's perched on a stool, biting into a red apple.

'Hello, mate.' Popeye winks.

'You look a bit peaky,' Mum says. 'You're not coming down with something, are you, Ricky?'

'No, I'm fine.'

She's always worrying that I'll get ill or nagging me about my asthma pump which is lost in the junk under my bed.

As I run upstairs, I realise an angel is sitting in my kitchen. My English teacher says when you're writing creatively to think of a first line that grabs your reader. 'An angel is sitting in my kitchen' would be my first line – only this is reality, not fiction.

Taking off my school uniform, I frown at my skinny body and the scrawny places where muscles should be. No wonder Justine Redd didn't call. My heart sinks – I'm only ever going to pull pity with a body like this.

Standing in front of the wardrobe mirror, I stare into my own eyes and wonder if I've been hallucinating, losing the plot. Mum's cousin Wilbert was in Friern Barnet psychiatric hospital for a while; he threw himself in the River Lea over by Tottenham Marshes and was dragged out by a couple of joggers. Mr McNamara, my science teacher, told our class that genes are complex things and you never know when or how they'll pop up; a bit of damaged, messed-up wiring or tough times and anyone can have psychiatric problems. But I think I'm sane. Popeye's an angel, earthbound and on a mission.

At the bottom of the stairs, Mum and Popeye wait, holding hands.

'You're both coming over to my place tonight. On the menu, Spag Bol à la Popeye – my treat,' Popeye says, and Mum laughs, her eyes mellow and moony when she looks at him.

'Great,' I say, a goofy smile on my face. What else do you say to an angel?

The lift's working and we travel up to Popeye's flat. The place is modern; chrome, glass and black waxy leather. There's a smell of onions and garlic, and underneath, the faint pong of sweaty trainers. It's hard to think of Popeye as divine when he has smelly trainers, but according to Wikipedia, angels are sacred, supernatural beings – though totally different from the demons who stalk Edmonton Green, according to Kev.

There are two large wooden carvings on the living room walls I haven't noticed before. One is of a Rastafarian man with closed eyes and long dreadlocks. The other is the shape of Jamaica and has a bright yellow ackee fruit painted at the top. I haven't been to Jamaica; I'd prefer to orbit around Sirius or, better still, have a look inside Heaven.

Popeye passes round a plate of warm garlic bread rolls and I take one. In the past, I would have taken two, but things are different now and I have to remember my manners.

'So, how's school?' Popeye asks.

'Science is great. We've done renewable energy, space and time, radioactivity. Mr McNamara's something else.'

'He sounds cool. If my science teachers were any good, I'd be an astronaut today.'

Mum laughs. She eats more slowly and keeps wiping her mouth with a napkin.

After dinner, Popeye stands and claps his hands.

'Now for the best bit, folks. Stay right here. I've got something to show you.'

He races into a back room and I can hear him moving things around, drawers opening and closing. When he comes back, Mum's finished her wine and I've scoffed another roll.

'Ta-da!' Popeye holds out a small cardboard box. 'Go on, open it,' he says to Mum.

Lifting the lid, she pulls out a sleek silver pen and looks up at Popeye.

'No, not just a pen,' he says. 'A James Bond pen. It's got a camera and a sound recorder inside.'

Popeye holds it up to the light.

'Say something,' he says.

'Hello? Anyone there? Great wine. Ha!' Mum says. Popeye presses a tiny button on the pen's side and Mum's voice is repeated.

There's a light click; Popeye's taken a photograph. A small square slides back. The shot shows Mum blinking and me staring back with red eyes. What would Kev make of this?

'Hmm, I'm not happy with the red eyes. Something needs fixing.' Popeye frowns.

My research didn't give me any clues as to how earthbound angels are created. I'm not sure if they all come from Heaven or somewhere else, or if one day people find themselves promoted, having grown wings. I've seen Popeye, T-shirt off, jogging round the Farm, but I haven't noticed any dents or marks where wings could sprout. I'll talk with Kev first thing in the morning; he'll join the dots.

'There's something else,' Popeye says. 'Now this is very, very special.'

Popeye disappears for a full half hour. Mum keeps leaning over and patting my hands until I move them out of reach and keep them under the dining table.

'I'm not drunk,' she says. 'Just merry.' I groan. I think she's in love.

There are clanking and thumping noises as Popeye clomps down the hall. When he steps into the living room, strapped to his back is a metal box with switches and levers. Mum covers her mouth with her hands, her eyes bulging like gobstoppers.

'This took me two years to develop,' Popeye says. 'I bought some gear over the net from Japan and just mucked around. I've revamped, tweaked, replaced – and now it really works.'

Large white wings made of wire mesh and feathers spring from the box.

'What is it exactly?' Mum asks.

'It's a flying machine,' I hear myself say. My heart sinks to the floor. Mechanical wings. Fricking mechanical wings.

'Exactly. How d'you work that out, Ricky?' Popeye asks, his dark eyes twinkling. He watches my face.

'Predicted A stars in physics, chemistry and biology,' says Mum before I can answer.

'Yes, our Ricky is an extremely bright boy,' Popeye says.

He moves closer and in a quiet voice says, 'I've got a meeting next week with a NASA rep. They're interested in buying the patent, but we've got to keep this under wraps, okay? Top secret.'

The wings retract and a rock lodges in my throat.

Reaching for the bottle of wine, Mum shakes her head. 'Unbelievable. Are you for real, Popeye? I'm going out with the Nutty Professor, Ricky... Can I have a go when it's up and running?'

Popeye gives me another wink, but I'm not sure of its meaning and I go silent for the rest of the evening.

As Mum and I walk home, a few boys do wheelies on their bikes and nod as we pass. The moon's not bright tonight, the stars snuffed out by low-lying clouds.

'Can you believe that, Ricky? A flying machine?'

I don't say anything.

'What's wrong with you? Why have you gone all quiet, and what's the face for? I thought you'd be in your element with all Popeye's science stuff...' She shakes her head. 'I dunno what to make of you sometimes, Ricky Thompson.'

As Mum opens the front door, we walk into a wall of thick, warm air.

'Oh no,' she says. 'I've only gone and left the central heating on.'

Shoving her feet into her slippers, she mumbles about having a head like a sieve. I trudge upstairs and flop on my bed while a fit Beyonce looks down from the ceiling. She doesn't look too pleased either. I don't want to think, but thoughts come anyway. Non-stop what ifs buzz around my brain, offering no answers. I decide I've got two options; I can choose to believe Popeye is a BT engineer who has invented a flying machine, or I can believe he's an angel who caught me watching him the other night and has made up a cover story to hide his true identity.

Tucked under my duvet, I reach out and turn off the small bedside light. Pressing against the window is the night sky. I know the names of the planets above the clouds. I've read about dark matter, black holes and turbulence. Tiny and I are flip sides of the same coin, both raised on the Farm, both reaching for the stars – but Tiny's wrong; the Farm's not a sinking ship. There is always hope. A grin flits across my face; I've got choices. I won't be a runner or a lookout. Things can change. Is Popeye an angel or an inventor? I know what Kev would say.

I decide to watch again to see if things have changed, and I wait and wait until, just before 3am, Popeye's balcony doors open. Slowly he steps onto the edge of the balcony and balances. There are no contraptions tied to his back. As he waves his arms, two large, feathery white wings spring from his body and he launches upwards, leaping from the balcony and flying into the black face of the night sky.

He twirls and spins, carving lines of golden light that leave a sparkling ribbon behind him. Moving with growing speed, he soars deeper into the sky until he fades into the darkness. Popeye is gone for the longest forty minutes I've ever known and then, like a tiny dot, his figure reappears. Speeding towards the Farm, he dips and dives. Closer and closer he flies, and I'm just about to duck to avoid being seen when his figure stops and hovers close to my window. Looking straight across at me, Popeye gives me a smile and a thumbs up, before gliding back to his flat on the seventeenth floor of Northolt block. Change is coming.

AUTHOR'S NOTE

In 1985 Broadwater Farm erupted across the front pages of our newspapers with coverage of the riots and the tragic deaths of Cynthia Jarrett and PC Keith Blakelock. Further riots in 2011, sparked by the fatal shooting of Mark Duggan, added to the image of Broadwater Farm as deeply troubled. Discourse centred around policing, racism, criminality, poverty, education, housing and the hard truths of growing up in Tottenham and inner cities.

The stories in *Broadwater* are set in Tottenham and north London. The region continues to evolve, and the stories reflect those changes and the challenges associated with them.

These stories are about ordinary people struggling with the everyday complexities and realities of life. Characters 'cope and hope' within the context of contemporary London.

Broadwater Farm itself is turning around; no longer defined by its troubled past, it is looking forward to the future. Recent crime statistics show a decrease in overall crime rates and the robberies and serious assaults rates were virtually nil in 2005, making Broadwater Farm one of the safest areas in which to live within Haringey.

Although some challenges remain, there is a growing sense of an energised and united community committed to an optimistic future where its young people are not defined by a problematic past or negative, stigmatising folklore.

Broadwater explores universal conflicts, dreams and losses that we all share as human beings, regardless of demographic tags or location.

Broadwater was completed during the Coronavirus pandemic – a period of global, national and local devastation and challenge. This is also a time of contradiction; of lockdown and quiet, yet also a time of disquiet and disturbance. Within this crisis, however, we have a gift, a unique opportunity to co-create a more compassionate and wiser way of relating and living. I hope that we will each find the courage and resolve to be part of the change, healing and recovery that are needed and hoped for.

ACKNOWLEDGEMENTS

Sincere thanks to those mentioned below, without whom *Broadwater* would not exist:

My editor, Urška Vidoni, whose wise counsel and insight were invaluable, and the rest of the wonderful Fairlight Books team, who were with me every step of the way.

My family – Selvyn, Ina, Gary and Vilma Thompson, and Alicia Thompson and Michael Redican.

My cousins and uncles and aunts, especially Adlin Graham, Barbara Harris and Maureen O'Sullivan. The villages of Silver Grove and Bounty Hall, Jamaica, and the magnificent Harris and Thompson families.

For your unwavering belief in my writing – Angel White, Paul Coleman, Diana Evans, Tony Crittenden, Louis Joseph, Onjali Rauf, Paul Williams, Maron Ashley, Tracy Antoniou, Pat Plant, David Austin, Nick Bedford and the Kaczmar family.

My William Forster School (now Parkview Academy) family, our former teachers and my Face Front Inclusive Theatre family.

Loved ones – Chris Penny, Oren Coleman and Anthony Crittenden.

Inspiring young people – Lauren Pell, Malachi Bakas, Cannadine Boxill-Harris, Renell Mckenzie-Lyle and Ayleah Dawn Thompson-Findley.

The Sophie Warne Foundation, The Leather Lane Writers Group, The Winston Churchill Memorial Trust, The Bridport Prize and Birkbeck University Creative Writing Department, both lecturers and former students.

And finally, to all former and present residents of Broadwater Farm and the people of Tottenham.

ABOUT THE AUTHOR

Jac Shreeves-Lee is a short story author who was born and bred in Tottenham. Her pieces have been widely published in various anthologies, including Virago, the Mechanics Institute Review and the Bridport Prize Anthology 2017. Jac's stories have been shortlisted for the Bridport Prize and longlisted for the Fish Publishing Prize. Jac gained a distinction in her MA Creative Writing course from Birkbeck University. She is currently working as a clinical psychologist and a magistrate.

Broadwater is her debut collection of short stories.

Bookclub and writers' circle notes for
Broadwater can be found at
www.fairlightbooks.com

FAIRLIGHT BOOKS

HELEN STANCEY

The Madonna of the Pool

'*I do not cheat others. Have I cheated myself? I do not know who I am.*'

The Madonna of the Pool is a collection of short stories which explore the triumphs, compromises and challenges of everyday life. Drawing on a wide array of characters, Helen Stancey shows how small events, insignificant to some, can resonate deeply in the lives of others.

Richly poetic, deeply moving and entirely engaging, these short stories demonstrate an exquisite understanding of human adaptation, endurance and, most of all, optimism.

'*Stancey has pieced together a collection that feels subtle and truthful to the human experience.*'
— *The Book Bag*

'*One has a sense of a writer gifted with an instinctive sense of how to tell a story.*'
— *The Spectator*

AMI RAO

David and Ameena

David and Ameena *takes a profoundly insightful
look into the lives of two people, brought together
by their dreams and the city they inhabit.*

Modern-day New York, a subway train. David, an American-Jewish jazz musician, torn between his dreams and his parents' expectations, sees a woman across the carriage. Ameena, a British-Pakistani artist who left Manchester to escape the pressure from her conservative family, sees David.

When a moment of sublime beauty occurs unexpectedly, the two connect, moved by their shared experience. From this flows a love that it appears will triumph above all. But as David and Ameena navigate their relationship, their ambitions and the city they love, they discover the external world is not so easy to keep at bay.

'*I've never read such an accurate and telling
evocation of the additional complications of
personal creative expression.*'
— Tim Hayward, writer,
broadcaster and columnist

SOPHIE VAN LLEWYN

Bottled Goods

*Longlisted for **The Women's Prize for Fiction 2019**,*
***The Republic of Consciousness Prize 2019** and*
The People's Book Prize 2018

When Alina's brother-in-law defects to the West, she and her husband become persons of interest to the secret services and both of their careers come grinding to a halt.

As the strain takes its toll on their marriage, Alina turns to her aunt for help – the wife of a communist leader and a secret practitioner of the old folk ways.

Set in 1970s communist Romania, this novella-in-flash draws upon magic realism to weave a captivating tale of everyday troubles.

'Sophie van Llewyn's stunning debut novella
shows us there is no dystopian fiction as
frightening as that which draws on history.'
— Christina Dalcher, author of *VOX*

'Sophie van Llewyn has brought light into an
era which cast a long shadow.'
— Joanna Campbell, author of
Tying Down the Lion